Samurai Spirit

Samurai Spirit

Ancient Wisdom for Modern Life

by

BURT KONZAK

Tundra Books

Published in Canada by Tundra Books,
481 University Avenue, Toronto, Ontario M5G 2E9

Published in the United States by Tundra Books of Northern New York,
P.O. Box 1030, Plattsburgh, New York 12901

Library of Congress Control Number: 2002103703

National Library of Canada Cataloguing in Publication Data

Konzak, Burt, 1946-
Samurai spirit : ancient wisdom for modern life / Burt Konzak.

ISBN 0-88776-611-0

1. Samurai – Juvenile fiction. I. Title.

PS8571.O728S24 2002   jC813'.54   C2002-901395-X
                         PZ7

We acknowledge the support of the Canada Council for the Arts and the
Ontario Arts Council for our publishing program.

We acknowledge the financial support of the Government of Canada
through the Book Publishing Industry Development Program for our
publishing activities.

Design: Blaine Herrmann

Printed and bound in Canada

1 2 3 4 5 6   07 06 05 04 03 02

To my daughters, Sonya and Mélina,
who have been the inspiration for each story,
and whose enthusiasm to learn
has filled the lives of those around them
with meaning and wonder

ACKNOWLEDGMENTS

I would like to express my sincere appreciation to Kat Mototsune, editor, and to Kathy Lowinger, Publisher of Tundra Books, who have contributed immensely to the development of this book, both by their enthusiasm and their useful ideas. I would also like to thank Blaine Herrmann in the art department of McClelland & Stewart, and Alison Morgan and Catherine Mitchell in the promotions department of Tundra for all their effort and creativity.

My students at the Toronto Academy of Karate have been wonderfully supportive of the samurai spirit and have contributed many fantastic ideas. I have been truly fortunate to have such friends and students, and I value them every day.

My wife, Françoise, and daughters, Sonya and Mélina, have over the years spent many evenings patiently listening to dinner-time samurai stories and have helped me to select the best for this book. What is truly best is that they have shared a passion for martial arts and samurai ideals with me. Without their support, this book, and my life, would never be the same. *Merci*.

CONTENTS

It is proper to doubt.
People tell you one thing. And others tell you another.
But when you realize that something is unwholesome
and bad for you, give it up.
And when you realize that something is wholesome
and good for you, do it.

– Siddhartha Gautama (Buddha)

Introduction

The good warrior knows how important it is
to share his experience with others.
He evokes with enthusiasm the Path,
recounts how he has resisted a provocation,
what solution he has found for a difficult situation.
When he relates these stories,
he does so with passion and romance . . .
And with a condition to never confuse pride and vanity!

– Paulo Coelho (author's adaptation)

The soul of the samurai is a spirit that can never be defeated, a dream that can never be extinguished. The brilliance of the samurai vision is expressed in a tradition of stories that emphasize personal training and development. These artists and warriors created a literature that transforms and inspires us to conquer our fears and insecurities and to be our best.

When I was a teenager, I had no idea that I'd ever study the martial arts, but I loved to read stories about samurai. I was attracted by their sheer energy and the way they related to my own life. In a society where there seems to be rules for everything, somehow the samurai I read about were able to find a way to express themselves. I think all teens at times feels this desire to "break on through," and that is why samurai imagery, fierce and furious, is so appealing.

Samurai stories told me about people who faced impossible challenges, people who met those challenges with their inner resources more often than with physical strength. They inspired me to think for myself and to understand that no truth taught to me by others means anything if it cannot be experienced by myself in my own heart. Eventually they led me to the martial arts and to Asian philosophy, and turned me onto a path that I have never abandoned.

Most importantly, I learned that we can make every single minute count by appreciating every moment. The stories often had to do with life-or-death situations, but they made it clear that life – no matter how hard it might be at the moment – is very precious, and worth fighting for.

I hope that you will love these stories as much as I did – and still do – and that they will be a source of strength and encouragement to you when you face your own challenges. I have told these stories many times over the years, and in the telling they have changed. Great stories are part of an oral tradition, so they grow and change to reflect the times they are told in. But they are not simply a reflection of life; they can alter life by helping us make changes in the way we live. I've learned a lot about the way I am from these stories, and I've also found characters who have shown me ways I'd like to be. There are enough role models here to last a lifetime!

I
The Samurai Spirit

*A person who has attained mastery of a martial art
reveals it in his every action.*

– Samurai proverb

THE SAMURAI'S THREE SONS

Hundreds of years ago, there lived in Japan a master samurai, Matsuta Bokuden. He was known as a brave and talented warrior. So skilled and quick was he that he once thwarted an attack from behind without even turning his head!

Alas, Bokuden, fine warrior and caring teacher, was growing old. The challenges of running his martial arts school, his *dojo*, were becoming burdensome. The time had come to pass on the leadership to someone younger.

Bokuden had three sons, each a powerful fighter and mighty samurai. He wondered which of his sons would be

3

the best *sensei*, or teacher, for his school. When he spoke of his quandary, people laughed.

"There is no question," they would tell him. "The oldest always takes over from the father. It is tradition."

"Tradition is important," Bokuden would reply. "But it should not be the only star that lights our way. We have to think each problem through."

And questions did nag at him. Would his oldest son be the best *sensei* – just because he was the oldest? Was it fair for the students to have a *sensei* whose main qualification was just that – that he was the oldest? Would one of his other sons, perhaps more dedicated to the martial arts, resent being passed over by a brother for no other reason – just that he was the oldest?

All of Bokuden's sons were excellent martial artists, it was true. But Bokuden knew that physical strength by itself does not give one mastery of the martial arts, or of any part of life. He wanted to look beyond fast hands or swift feet.

Bokuden was a man of action. He knew that thoughts without action are empty. He believed that his *dojo* deserved the best master, whether or not that man was the oldest. He had to put his beliefs to the test.

"Yamamoto, please come join me," said Bokuden one day to his assistant, the highest ranking samurai in the *dojo* after the master himself. He had been with Bokuden as long as anyone could remember. Bokuden had been Yamamoto's first teacher, and Yamamoto had been Bokuden's first student. Although younger than Bokuden, he was not nearly as spry as the old master and had lost much of his strength and flexibility.

Yamamoto wished his master had not decided to retire,

and he feared for the future of the *dojo*. He knew each potential successor had his own devoted followers among the student body. It would not be the first time that a *dojo* would be divided into factions when the master died or retired. If the eldest son did not carry the respect of the other samurai, many would leave to establish a new *dojo*. Yamamoto wished that Bokuden would at least delay such a possibility by staying on as *sensei* as long as he could still move.

"Each of my sons has different talent," explained Bokuden. "I will devise a test to see who is best suited to be the next *sensei*. Let us see whose talents will serve him best."

Yamamoto was relieved that Bokuden had a plan. It was true that each of the boys was very different. Bokuden's youngest was extremely strong, with big muscles that he exercised each day. Some said they had seen him cutting down trees with a single swing of his sword. Bokuden's middle son was not nearly as strong, but he was fast as a hawk. He could block a blow and retaliate in the wink of an eye. He could leap high into the air to avoid a sweeping strike with the sword. Often he would land behind his opponent with such speed that he seemed nothing but a blur in the air. Bokuden's oldest son was neither as strong as the youngest nor as swift as the middle brother, but he had such concentrated focus it was unnerving. The students talked of sparring with him, of deciding which part of his body to attack, only to find that he had blocked their punch before they had even moved.

"Your sons are all fine martial artists," said Yamamoto. "How will you test them?"

"Let's place a pillow over the curtain at the entrance to the room. We'll arrange it so that the slightest touch will make it fall on the head of anyone who enters." Once Bokuden had arranged the test as he described it, he sent Yamamoto to call his youngest son.

Yamamoto found the boy flexing his massive biceps. "Come with me," he said. "Your father wishes to see you."

Youngest Son was quick to obey his father. He hurried after Yamamoto. When he reached the *dojo*, he swept aside the curtain to enter the room. *Plop.* The pillow landed with a soft thud on the back of his neck.

Youngest Son was enraged by the pillow attack. He drew his sword and cut the pillow into pieces before it could even reach the floor. The *dojo* filled with a cloud of feathers. Bokuden and Yamamoto sneezed as the youngest son waved his hands in front of him, trying to disperse the wall of feathers floating in front of his face.

"My son," began Bokuden. He sneezed again. "Must you always overpower everything, even a pillow?"

"If that pillow had been an attacker," he said to his father, "I would have cut him into a thousand pieces."

"If that pillow had been an attacker," his father responded, "you would already have been dead. Block first. Then attack. All the strength in the world is useless if your opponent gets in the first strike. You must work harder to anticipate danger if you are to defend yourself."

Knowing he had displeased his father, Youngest Son stormed from the room. "He does not understand," said Bokuden, saddened by the realization.

The old master found another pillow and arranged it over the entryway while Yamamoto swept up the feathers. When the room was clean, he sent Yamamoto to call his middle son, saying, "Let us hope he can do better."

A few minutes later, a slim young man slid through the entryway. With a soft *whoosh* the pillow fell, but Middle Son was quick. He caught it deftly in his hands. Then he turned toward his father and smiled. "Good morning," he said. "How are you, Father?"

"Very well," Bokuden answered, relieved that Middle Son had shown himself to be both agile and composed. Bokuden felt that the family's honor had been at least partly re-established.

Then it was the turn of his eldest son. The moment Eldest Son arrived at the entranceway, he noticed the pillow resting on the curtain rod. He took it down, walked under the curtain rod, plumped the pillow, and put it back in its original position.

"Good morning, Sensei," he said as he bowed to his father.

"Eldest Son, how did you see the pillow?" asked Bokuden.

"I saw it because it was there. You taught me that a samurai is always aware of his surroundings, whether it is a sunset or an attacker hidden in a dark alley. When we are training in the *dojo*, you always tell us that the mind of a martial artist must be ever alert. So I saw the pillow. I hope you don't mind that I took it down before it fell. I thought you must have put it there for a reason."

"Eldest Son, you are an excellent samurai and well qualified to be *sensei*." With that, Bokuden passed to his first son his own ceremonial sword. "You will be the new *sensei*, not simply because you are the eldest, but because you understand what it means to be a great samurai."

Who Were the Samurai?

The samurai were the members of the Japanese warrior class for 700 years. They took great pride in their military skills and in their disciplined lifestyle. Their martial abilities became legendary throughout the world, and they are still considered to be consummate warriors. Not limited to fighting, samurai culture developed many unique Japanese arts – including the tea ceremony, flower arranging, and poetry – that are practiced to this day. Traditional samurai training stressed moral and intellectual education, as well as personal refinement and appreciation of beauty in nature. The traditional samurai was supposed to be brave, honorable, and loyal. All these aspects of the samurai spirit made up *bushido*, the way of the warrior. The word *samurai* means "one who serves," and the samurai warrior considered himself essential to the protection of his community and to his country, ready to sacrifice his very life if necessary.

There are samurai to this day. A modern-day samurai is a person who draws inspiration from the wisdom and accomplishments of the ancient ways: a person who appreciates the beauty of life and the tiny everyday miracles of nature; a person who knows that every moment in life deserves his or her best efforts. Modern-day samurai do not carry swords or weapons. Nor do they, for the most part, engage in physical battles. They battle within themselves to overcome the enemies that can stand in the way of really living: laziness, a lack of self-discipline, fear of fear. And when they are called to do it, they stand up and support others who need their help.

THE SWORD OF BEAUTY AND
THE SWORD OF DEATH

An elderly samurai was walking alone down the dark empty streets of Nara, the capital city of the island of Okinawa. He had just visited a friend who lived in the poorer, run-down section of town. As he walked, he gazed intently at the full moon. *It's odd*, he thought, *how people fear the full moon and the dark legends that surround it*. He remembered the words of his late *sensei*: "The light of the moon flows everywhere. Be like the moon that shines its light on every lake and river without discrimination. Thus should our minds be. We must develop *tsuki-no-kokoro* (a mind like the moon), which shines its light and beauty everywhere."

As he walked down the narrow street, he heard footsteps behind him. It was the sound of someone trying not to make a sound. It was the sound of a large man, moving fast. The old samurai tightened his back and stomach muscles, but he did not change his pace. Suddenly, he felt a *whoosh* through the air. He dodged to the right and caught the man's fist in his armpit. Still he did not slow his steps. Instead, he dragged his attacker, now pulled off-balance, through the street with him, twisting the attacker's wrist as he walked. All this without even turning around.

The attacker squirmed from pain and begged to be released. The old man turned his head to look into the eyes of his attacker. He recognized the man from a demonstration of martial arts they had both engaged in. He was part of a new *dojo* that had recently opened.

"I will be happy to release you – once you tell me why you attacked me."

"My *sensei* encouraged me to do so in order to prove that your *dojo* is not as good as ours."

"I see," the older man mused. "That way you can get all the students. But you should not go around playing tricks like that on old men." So saying, he did as he promised and released the younger man.

The would-be assailant glared at the older samurai but didn't dare attack again. After all, even with the advantages of surprise and the cover of darkness on his side, he hadn't managed to succeed in his first attack.

"You are clearly very strong," the old samurai said. "I imagine you thought you were quiet, too."

"But I was!" the young man protested.

"Yet I heard you. Do you know why? An alert mind defeats stealth and muscle every time. You will be a much better person for being aware of every detail. Learn to carry the sword that creates beauty, not the sword that sows death."

The old samurai calmly resumed his walk home, turning his eyes once again to the beauty of the moon and his memories of his old master.

The Best Samurai: Musashi Miyamoto

Musashi Miyamoto (1584–1645) grew up in a poor family in a small village in a very class-conscious socirty. By the strength of his spirit, he became the greatest samurai in the history of Japan. A soldier-artist, he combined all the traits of a full samurai: thinking deep thoughts as a philosopher, writing elegant verse, disciplining his mind and body as a warrior. He was as famous for his art – powerful paintings, wooden sculptures, and beautiful sword guards in metal – as he was for his expertise in battle. He is best known for having written *A Book of Five Rings*, a bestseller in Japan since the seventeenth century. This classic examination of strategy and samurai spirit became a bestseller in North America, too, when people applied its philosophy to business strategy in the 1970s.

A samurai must have both literary and martial skills.
To be versed in the two is his duty.
The samurai pursues martial arts in order to excel in everything. . . .
The true spirit of martial arts trains you in many ways
not limited to the sword.
If you acquire expertise only in swordsmanship,
you will never see the way of the warrior.

– Musashi Miyamoto, *A Book of Five Rings*

Musashi Miyamoto is not considered the best simply because he was a great warrior. By his own account, there were others greater than he. His place in history rests on the broad dimensions of his accomplishments – what he would call *bunbu-ryodo* (combining martial and intellectual training).

Musashi knew an important truth: more important than being the best was knowing how to be the best he could be. And now, more than four hundred years later, that's still good enough!

II
The Way of the Warrior
---*---

Be like water,
the most gentle and yielding of all substances.
Yet what is stronger than water,
which shapes valleys and rivers?
A rock gets in its way,
and the water goes around it.
A thousand years later, the rock is but sand,
and the water flows in its place.

– adapted from Lao-tsu

THE FIGHT

Four of us were walking through a dark, hot summer night to a party in Cedarhurst. Mary, the girl who was having the party, lived in a beautiful house on the other side of the tracks from where I lived in Far Rockaway. To get there, we had to walk through Rockaway's roughest neighborhood.

The damp ocean air hung heavily in the summer night. We passed a brightly lit fire station, which gave us a sense of security. Two firemen wearing heavy boots and pants with suspenders sat outside the doorway. I felt very much a kid next to them. "Not too far to go," I thought as I waved at one of the firemen. He waved back.

A bright blue Oldsmobile pulled up next to us, and a tall older guy, about twenty, leaned out the window to ask where we were going.

"Nowhere," I said "Just walking."

"No way," he said. "Four punks like you dressed up like that. You're going to a party. Tell me where it is."

"We're just out walking," I insisted. "It's a nice night." The courage of the firemen must have rubbed off on me.

It didn't take more than two seconds for the tall guy and his five friends to pile out of the car and come at me. I looked confidently at the firehall. The stoop was empty. The firemen had gone inside. My friends had backed away around the corner. I was alone – fourteen years old and dressed in my best clothes – against six of the biggest goons I had ever seen.

What seemed like hours of punches and kicks later, I lay bleeding on the sidewalk. Through the mist in my eyes, I saw them walking back to their car, pleased with themselves. I guess beating me up was more fun than crashing the party that I suffered so much to defend from them.

I saw the boots of the firemen approaching me. They helped me up, took me inside, and washed the blood from my face. It was then that my friends reappeared. Shaken, we continued walking to the party.

When we arrived at Mary's house, she took a washcloth and cleaned the blood from my white shirt, as everyone watched. I was beginning to understand that I was in the process of becoming a hero – at least for one night. Not bad for someone who lost!

"How will you explain this to your mother?" she asked. I suddenly felt very unheroic.

"I don't know."

"Thanks for not telling them where you were going."

"I couldn't. It would be terrible if they crashed your party. I just had no idea how difficult it would be to say 'no,'" I admitted.

"Are you sorry you did?"

How could I answer that? To Mary, for that night, I was someone special. That made a real difference to me. I felt less stupid. And I knew I had done the right thing. I wasn't sorry for what I had done. The problem was that I didn't have the strength to back up my convictions in a practical way. I looked forward to being stronger someday, and not just fourteen and helpless.

$$\mathcal{H}$$

I had no idea where these thoughts would lead me.

My father said I should take up boxing. As if boxing would have helped against those six goons! My mother immediately vetoed that, saying I should spend more time on my studies to do better in school. That was her standard speech: I should spend my time studying.

In fact, I didn't mind studying. I knew I had to if I wanted to go to university and one day move to a different (and safer) neighborhood. I was getting tired of the constant humidity and salt air of Far Rockaway.

I dreamed of being a scientist – perhaps a biochemist or a marine biologist. I also liked philosophy. And I loved reading, particularly about Japan.

How did I become interested in Japan? Well, in one sense, it was because I loved sports. It sounds like a strange connection, doesn't it? But, you see, much as I loved sports, they also seemed pointless to me. It was always "win at all costs." You didn't build your body; you spent more effort destroying it – especially in football. I played football for many years and decided, after almost tearing my knees, that I might need them for better things later in life. When I was knocked out cold in one game, my mother told me that I might find a better use for my head, too, someday!

I longed for a physical activity that had more to it than simply winning a game. I wasn't interested in how my team measured up to some other team. I was interested in how I measured up today to the way I was yesterday.

Then I read about the martial arts, the training system of the samurai. It developed strength but also character. Now that would be worth doing! I searched for a martial arts school, but in those days there were not many around – certainly not in Far Rockaway. It would be years before I would find a school, and even longer before I would find one where I would want to study. As I quickly discovered, even in the martial arts with its tradition and history of character development, many people were in it for the violence. Rather than self-defence, their activities were all about what I would call self-offence. It was truly offensive to themselves, and even more so to others. So I contented myself with reading about the martial arts and the samurai spirit. Perhaps most importantly, I learned the type of *dojo* that I wanted to find. And although it took me years, I found it.

What Are the Martial Arts?

Many people believe that the Asian martial arts are essentially a superlative form of fighting, but they are much more than that. From Japanese *karate-do*, *judo*, and *aikido*, to Chinese *wu-shu*, to Korean *tae kwon do*, they all are rooted in a philosophy of self-development based on physical exercise, with origins in the breathing and meditation techniques of yoga. The martial arts are based on the principle of harmony between the mind and body, and the development of a strong spirit. They are also founded on respect – as students of the martial arts, we all bow as we enter the *dojo*. The ideal of training is not to defeat others, but to conquer our own fear, weakness, and lack of will. With confidence, with grace, and with dignity, we learn to diffuse aggression and to handle every challenge with flexibility, understanding, and kindness.

THE WANDERER IN THE JUNGLE

*Imposing one's will on another is a
demonstration of ordinary strength.
Imposing one's will on oneself
attests to true power.*

– Lao-tsu

Twenty-five hundred years ago in India, Siddhartha Gautama, the Buddha, sat in meditation deep in the forest.

A group of people, wandering through the trees, came upon him. One of the men in the group was very wealthy. The night before, he had been out drinking, had met a woman, and had taken her back to his house. When he awoke, she was gone. Also gone were his money and valuables. When he discovered the theft, he ran to get his neighbors. They joined him in furious pursuit of the woman. Thus it was that a rowdy, noisy, and somewhat drunken group had gathered.

This was the crowd who came across the Buddha in the forest. They were thrilled. They had chanced upon the most famous spiritual teacher in all of India. They were anxious to garner some wisdom from the sage. They asked him many questions, and the Buddha patiently responded to all of them.

He was not, however, unaware of their drunken condition. He asked them how it was that they found themselves wandering in the dangerous forest.

The wealthy man who had gathered the group explained the whole story without hesitation. The Buddha asked if this type of thing happened often.

"No," the rich man answered, "it is not that common for a courtesan to steal your money."

But the Buddha explained that what he meant was this: "Does it happen very often you spend your time drinking and chasing after women?"

"Yes, of course," the rich man replied. "That's what we do with our time and money."

"I see," said the Buddha.

The group asked if the Buddha had any advice for them. Did he know of a place where the woman might be hiding?

"Which is better for you?" the Buddha responded. "To wander around in a dangerous jungle, full of wild beasts and poisonous insects, looking for a woman and some stolen money, or to discover yourselves?"

They gave the Buddha bored looks, expecting a long lecture. It didn't come. What they received was a single question. "Wouldn't it be wiser to spend some effort searching for your true self – to find out who you really are, what you are capable of, and what you can accomplish in life?"

The man who had been robbed, recognizing the Buddha's understanding, intelligence, and own extraordinary example, had a moment of enlightenment. Suddenly his own existence – chasing after money, drink, and women – seemed meaningless.

He stayed in the forest and became a student of the Buddha.

Human beings worry about the past and fear for the future. Buddha placed an emphasis on self-discovery. Many people all through history have taken drugs to achieve this experience, but Buddha taught that it could be achieved naturally through training of the body and mind. He inspired the people wandering in the forest to develop their own capacities in order to lead an attentive life, moment by meaningful moment.

From Meditation to Martial Arts

Buddha's teachings spread all over Asia. Daruma was a Buddhist monk from India who, in the sixth century, traveled across the Himalayas to China. He brought with him an art that combined meditation and physical training. This meditation was physically dynamic, incorporating elements of self-defence that gave the practitioners a mental, spiritual, and physical power.

In time, what Daruma taught came to be called Zen Buddhism, or Zen. The Japanese word *zen* means meditation: *do-zen* is the active and dynamic practice of martial arts – moving meditation, learning to focus one's concentration and breathing while in action. Daruma was a devoted, demanding, and dynamic teacher. He led by his own example of unrelenting practice, which consisted of blocks, punches, and kicks to toughen up the spirits and bodies of his students. Daruma was strong. He made his students strong as well.

THE BUSINESS CARD

In a small town near Kyoto, an exceptional master of karate ran a *dojo* that was the pride of the province. The governor of the province often passed through this town and, being a practitioner of karate himself, he had always wished to visit this illustrious *dojo*.

One day, the governor finally had the opportunity to call upon the famous *sensei*. Upon entering the *dojo*, he gave his card to the attendant, who presented it to the *sensei*. The card read

Masa Okumura

Governor of Kyoto

"I do not know this man," the master of the *dojo* said when he read the card. "I have no interest in such a person. Tell him to go away."

The assistant returned to the office where the governor awaited him and apologetically passed on the response of the *sensei*.

The well-dressed visitor looked puzzled for a moment. Then he took his card back, crossed out the words *Governor of Kyoto*, and gave it back to the young man. "That was my error. Please ask your teacher again."

When the attendant brought the card once more to the *sensei*, he smiled and said, "Oh, it's Masa Okumura! Invite him in. I want to see him."

Martial Arts Spirit

The word *ki* or *chi* means "spirit." It also stands for energy and breath. In the martial arts, the *kiai* is the expression of the powerful abdominal muscles, the foundation of martial arts technique. Unlike a yell that comes from the throat, *kiai* comes from the abdomen, and is a deep breathing movement similar to the instinctive grunt we all make when exerting great force. Using the *ki* is what enables a person to defeat a much larger opponent in a graceful judo throw. It is what lies at the heart of a beautiful karate *kata*, or demonstration of technique, imbuing the dance-like movement with unbelievable power.

Beginners in martial arts training wear a white belt. As they progress, they are awarded darker belts: yellow, green, blue, purple, brown, and finally black. Over time, and with continued training, the black belt becomes frayed and worn; it becomes white. And so the highest honor is to be a white belt once again, to always approach training with the wonder and enthusiasm of a beginner.

Titles and status are left at the door when you study real martial arts. Perhaps this is one of the greatest gifts of the samurai spirit: to be simply yourself, not full of yourself.

For years, I continued my search for a good *dojo*, a place where I could learn the traditional values of the samurai, a school that taught not violence but character, that stressed building the mind and body, not the ego. And I finally did find one

"When you enter the *dojo* for the first time," my long-sought-after teacher explained to me on my very first day, "you bow at the door, say good-evening to Sensei, and take a deep breath – because your life will never again be the same."

THE FIGHT CONTINUED: THE CHOICE

It is not in lofty thoughts
but rather in solid actions
that real results are obtained.

– Martial arts aphorism

I left the *dojo* and walked across the gravel parking lot to catch the bus back to the university. I was seventeen and just finishing my freshman year. By that time, I had worked hard and held a blue belt in karate and judo. I was thoroughly drained after the workout, and the slight breeze was just cool enough that I was happy to be wearing my new leather university jacket.

Walking between the cars, three guys in surplus-store army jackets were cutting across the lot in front of me. One had long, red hair glistening in the glow of the full moon. I had a bad feeling and turned quickly to change my direction. But it was too late. I saw the punch coming straight at my head, fast and furious, as the redhead's two friends positioned themselves on either side of me.

I had spent the whole evening dodging faster punches than these, thrown by my teacher with enough force to knock me off my feet or to separate my nose from my face. The gravel shifted beneath my feet as I forcefully blocked the redhead's attack. I watched his face twitch as I thrust my fist hard into his solar plexus, sending him hunched over forward onto the ground, gasping for air.

To my great surprise, a second punch drove into my back from the guy who had positioned himself behind me as I blocked his comrade. My opponents were completely unafraid. What drugs were they on? Did they want my leather jacket that badly? I deflected the force of the blow by moving in the same direction as the punch was traveling, then spun around grabbing his hand, unbalancing him, and landing a solid elbow to his face. Two down, the third one standing on the sidewalk making mock kung-fu moves with a smile on his face. This wasn't about my jacket anymore – he was making fun of me!

Yet the third attacker obviously had no intention of ending up like his buddies. I wondered whether I should go after him. A part of me really wanted to give it to him, thinking of all the other kids these punks must have beaten into the ground and might terrorize in the future. I wanted to break them into pieces. I was hoping that he would attack me, giving me the justification to send him to the ground to join his friends. I even turned my back to give him an opening as I picked up my bag, but he was too savvy. He knew I could turn in a split second if he moved an inch. He stayed put.

I looked at the two groaning on the ground. I watched the third one, still playing his kung-fu moves while imitating my *kiai* in loud grunts as he kicked and punched the air. The three were beaten, but not sorry for what they had done. I wanted to punish them more. But what should I do – kick their ribs in, jump on their backs, and drive my heels into their spines while they were lying on the ground? I knew I couldn't. I knew I would not go after them. I would not become like them. Would my becoming a thug myself really accomplish anything? I had already taught them a lesson. They would always wonder whether that guy or girl they were about to attack was like me.

Certainly I had done better than when I was fourteen. I wouldn't want to live through that again, and I never will! It was a choice I had made. The real victory was in letting it go, not allowing the ego to get in the way. I walked home energized.

It doesn't take self-control to deal with situations in which everyone pleases you, where everything goes your way. That's easy. Situations that make you mad are what really challenge your character. Can you remain compassionate even in those circumstances? Can you still make the right choices in the heat of the moment? That is your real test as a samurai.

What do a Samurai's Swords Mean?

The sword is the soul of the samurai. In Japanese, the word for swordplay is *kendo*, which means the "path of the sword" or "the spiritual way of the sword." The image of the sword is present in all martial arts, not just *kendo*. The sword is seen not as an instrument of death, but as a tool of self-development, used to "cut out" the laziness, weakness, fear, hate, and anger within. At the same time, training in the martial arts builds discipline, strength, courage, sensitivity, and inner calm. Unlike the art of painting, with a brush as a tool for transforming a blank canvas, the martial art of *kendo* has a sword as a tool for transforming the blank canvas of the artist's own being. The samurai sculpts the body to be fit and capable, the mind to be focused and disciplined, and the spirit to be strong and indomitable.

THE SWORD OF VIOLENCE AND THE SWORD OF PEACE

Masamune was a legendary swordsmith, a master. His swords were, and still are, universally prized for their excellent qualities.

As far as the quality of the blade, a Masamune sword was no better than those made by his ablest disciple, Muramasa.

The difference had nothing to do with the metal. Masamune was said to instill his swords with something morally inspiring, something that came from within his very soul.

When testing the sharpness of a sword blade, a samurai would place the blade in a current of water and observe how it acted against the leaves floating downstream. Every leaf that met a Muramasa blade was instantly cut in two. But when a Masamune blade was tested in the same way, the leaves floated around the blade. The Masamune blade, just as sharp, was not bent on cutting. While the Muramasa blade excelled in destruction, the Masamune blade had true samurai spirit.

The Japanese sword reflects not only the swordsmith who created it, but also the samurai who carries it. A beautiful sword is considered a true work of art, not as a weapon of destruction, but an object of inspiration.

III
Tales of Wondrous Wisdom
—✳—

It is important to value the traditions of the martial arts,
but it is important to honor human life and dignity even more.
If a martial art pretends to be beneficial
but harms life or glorifies violence,
then it cannot be worthy.

– Meditation on the martial arts

THE FOX AND THE RABBIT

On a brisk autumn day, a martial arts *sensei* was walking in a field with one of his students. A rabbit ran past them, and not a few seconds later a red fox streaked after it.

"What a shame," said the student. "The rabbit is so beautiful, and now he is to die."

"Why will he die?" the master asked.

"The fox is so much faster and stronger," the student responded, surprised that his *sensei* would question what seemed so obvious.

"According to ancient wisdom, the rabbit will get away from the fox."

"But that cannot be," the student replied. "Look at how fast the fox is. He was like a bolt of lightning."

"Yet the rabbit will elude him."

"How can you be so certain?" asked the student, as the rabbit ran into the bush, the fox close on its heels.

A moment later the fox emerged from the bush. It circled and circled, and finally walked away, hungry, looking for new prey.

"Because the fox is running for his dinner, but the rabbit is running for his life," answered the master.

When there is an important challenge to overcome, we must put ourselves entirely into it, drawing upon our deepest strengths. We must be like the rabbit in this story, capable of outrunning even the stronger, swifter fox.

The rabbit does not always get away. But it has no chance at all if it doesn't try its hardest. In situations of crisis – a final exam, for example – some of us collapse, or become paralyzed by feelings of fear and inadequacy. Others rise to the occasion. As I often say to my martial arts students, as my teachers said to me, as passed on through generations going back to the ancient samurai: "Each of us has a choice. We alone can decide whether to be lions or lambs. That is the beauty of each of us being who we are – the power of our own free will to determine our destiny. We each have within us the power to be the masters of circumstances or their victims."

Life is not so simple. It is not merely a question of deciding that we will win in every situation. All around us good and strong people are defeated, and the weak and mean sometimes prosper.

But it is up to each one of us to find our own strength, to face life in the best way we can. It's not enough to have dreams. Dreams have to be realized by action. To become strong physically, we must exercise our bodies, develop muscle and suppleness. It is no less true of the mind and the spirit. The samurai realized this hundreds of years ago. Under the tutelage of Buddhist monks, they trained their minds and spirits to develop the same strength and suppleness as their muscles.

What is Ku-Fu?
The Japanese word *ku-fu* (*kung-fu* in Chinese) refers to the ability to summon up our deepest inner resources, toward the solution of a problem or the surmounting of a challenge. And this *ku-fu* comes from training – training in discipline, focus, determination, energy, flexibility, and inner strength.

THE SWORD OF STRENGTH vs
THE SWORD OF SPIRIT

Beneath the sword raised high
Hell makes you tremble
But by confronting it
You discover the land of bliss.

– Musashi Miyamoto

As a young samurai, Musashi Miyamoto traveled across Japan, perfecting his martial skills and acquiring as much combat experience as he could. But, over time, Musashi tired of conflict. He matured, becoming more interested in the moral issues of the martial arts. *How can one use one's martial spirit to construct a better world, instead of to destroy others?* He no longer sought duels with every noted swordsman he could find.

But swordsmen came seeking him out. They wanted the quick path to fame that would come with defeating the legendary samurai. Musashi would avoid fighting when it was possible to do so, and when it was not he would be careful to keep from killing or maiming his opponents. That did not stop them from coming at him with all their power. This hardly worried Musashi, who feared neither death nor his opponents.

Musashi did, however, desire to finish his life work. He

had become an accomplished painter and sculptor, seeking perfection in all he did as a culmination of the discipline of the martial arts. Each duel took him away from his work and his ideal of the martial artist in time of peace as a master of life instead of an instrument of death.

Gan-ryu was tall, elegant, and handsome, with large muscles and a long sword that only someone of his enormous strength and skill could control. That alone gave him the advantage over his opponents, who would quickly be cut down by Gan-ryu before they could get close enough to strike. He always smiled as he killed.

Musashi had once seen Gan-ryu duel. When Musashi fought, he was always focused on his opponent, breathing as his opponent breathed, feeling the flow of his opponent's movements, of his very thoughts. Gan-ryu's style was different. He was so relaxed in his stance that he looked almost as if he was asleep where he stood. Musashi was amazed at his smooth movements, his calm manner. In a few seconds the duel was over. A man lay dying on the ground, and Gan-ryu, smiling, walked over to greet Musashi.

"It is an honor to see you here," said Gan-ryu. "We must battle each other one day to see who is the greater samurai. I know your reputation. But, as you can see, I'm not so bad myself." Gan-ryu was perhaps the finest swordsman Musashi had ever seen.

Musashi congratulated Gan-ryu on his stunning victory and quickly turned to go back to his mountain retreat. He knew that one day Gan-ryu would come calling.

From that day, Musashi could not go anywhere without Gan-ryu appearing before him to challenge him to a match.

Musashi made excuses, but he knew that Gan-ryu would not give up. One day, Gan-ryu would tire of waiting. Sooner or later Musashi would have to fight.

When the match finally came to be, it was in a village beside a river. As Musashi knew he would, Gan-ryu did everything he could to force Musashi's hand. As he always did, Musashi refused. But Gan-ryu went to the governor of the province and offered him a tantalizing opportunity. What if one of the most important duels in Japanese history took place right in a little village in the governor's own province?

Gan-ryu had the governor post public notices of the impending match. Soon the word spread, and with it there was great excitement. Everyone was thrilled at the prospect of a great battle. How could even the poorest peasant not wish to see such an event? Musashi's fate was sealed. There was no way to refuse this time. The only thing left for Musashi to decide was the time and place, as was his right as the man being challenged.

"Sunrise on the island just east of the village," Musashi announced. Only one of the two men would return alive from that island. And everyone in the village thought that it would be the powerful Gan-ryu.

Musashi thought so too. He knew that it would take only a couple of moments for Gan-ryu to finish him off. Gan-ryu's calmness was his strength, Musashi calculated, but also perhaps a weakness. If a man's greatest strength lies in the power of his arm, and you can immobilize that arm, then you have a chance. Ah, but it was a lot easier to injure a man's arm than his calm. While Gan-ryu confidently practiced his technique, the more experienced Musashi did what he did best – he planned his strategy. He labored over every detail of the day that was to come.

In the stillness before dawn, as the eastern sky reddened, a flotilla of boats carried Gan-ryu's followers over the dark waters of the narrow channel separating the island, which was little more than a sandbar, from the village. Gan-ryu practiced on the beach, thrusting his sword, parrying, retreating, and then rapidly charging. His most famous move, of course, was that rapid charge, accompanied by a downward slice of his sword.

Gan-ryu knew that Musashi would be an opponent unlike any other he had faced, and he found himself looking expectantly across the waters to see if Musashi was approaching. He was anxious to get this day over with. A question popped into his head: *Could it be that I am afraid?* But he assured himself. *No, no. I am bigger, stronger, and fiercer. Look how easily I've always cut down my opponents.*

Gan-ryu had watched Musashi fight, just as Musashi had watched him. Musashi always looked as though the match were a deep personal struggle. It seemed as if his mental effort was as great as his physical effort. He was too intense, always plotting, always strategizing. No, Gan-ryu could not lose! How would it feel to be the man who finally killed the great Musashi? Soon he would know. For now, though, he reminded himself to concentrate on the technique, the great skill that would fell the famous samurai.

)(

While Gan-ryu practiced his kicks and punches, his sweeps and lunges on the sand, Musashi was still in his bed. Knowing that the day might be his last, he looked from his small window at the sun, just breaking over the horizon.

♓

Gan-ryu was growing impatient. Where was Musashi? Had he decided to run away? Could it be that the great Musashi had turned coward? The big samurai paced back and forth along the beach, looking over the water every few seconds, turning at every sound, expecting to see Musashi, sword drawn, charging at him. "Where is he?" he cried. Gan-ryu's followers assured him that his opponent was just late, that he would come. But Gan-ryu only grew more agitated. The sand felt cold under his feet and he grew tired of practicing, or even pretending to practice, as he paced back and forth along the beach. His arms were growing stiff from the morning cold and damp.

♓

Musashi finally arose and walked to the shore, searching for a boatman to take him across the channel. He found a smiling, strong fellow and climbed into his boat. The man recognized his famous passenger, and offered to row fast so that Musashi would not be too late.

"No," Musashi said. "Take your time. I want to enjoy the beauty of the sunrise. In fact, don't go directly. Row around the island and approach it from the other side, from the east."

"It will take a lot longer," the boatman explained. "You will arrive quite late."

Seeing a broken oar lying on the bottom of the boat, Musashi lifted it. "May I have this broken oar, if you no longer need it? I would like to carve something out of it."

"It would be an honor," the man replied proudly. "I have heard how beautifully you carve wood. May I watch you while I row?"

"Of course. And while I carve, I will admire the sun." As the boat glided through the water, Musashi thought about the fate that awaited him. Perhaps this would be his last sunrise, his last woodcarving, and his last pleasant conversation. The sun had never seemed so orange, the wood so pliant, or his companion so dear. "Perhaps I will die today."

"No, that is unimaginable. You are the great Musashi Miyamoto. You will never die!"

Musashi laughed. "Who do you think will win?"

"Gan-ryu is also great. You will have a tough fight."

"And who will win?"

"I am just a poor boatman. How can I say?"

"What does everyone else say?"

"What do they know?" the boatman scoffed.

"Ah, but I am not asking what they know, just what they say."

The boatman hesitated as he replied. "They all say that Gan-ryu is the stronger and that he will win."

"Yes, he is not only stronger, he is bigger and carries a longer sword. He also has incomparable skill."

"Yes, but you are still the mighty Musashi Miyamoto!"

"Nevertheless, in spite of your confidence, if I should die today, would you do me the service of bringing my body back to the village so that it doesn't rot on the island? I will pay you for the return trip now."

"Yes, sir. But today I believe I will bring you back still chattering with me, and dead men do not chatter."

Musashi fell silent, his eyes moving from the carving in his hands to the glorious sunrise, until the boat turned westward and approached the island. He felt the sun on his back, warming his shoulders and giving him the feeling of energy and optimism that only the sun can provide. He looked at the wooden sword that was taking shape in his hands. From a broken wooden oar, he had created a beautiful weapon. A weapon that might serve him well, he thought, fashioned by his own hands and heart while it gave him serenity at a time of great distress. The boatman's eyes glowed as he looked at it. How could a man facing death create something of such beauty?

The boatman knew nothing of the struggle going on within Musashi: a mind that had accepted the unity of life and death was at war with a body that felt the tingle of fear vibrate through every part. He carved the oar with great concentration. But it wouldn't be until he had reached full concentration and made peace within himself – giving up all thought, all purpose – that he would be fully ready for the challenge ahead. His eyes sparkled in the morning light, reflecting the sun on the water. Carving became effortless, flowing with the rhythm of the river. Musashi had completely become one with the sun and the water.

When they came to the island, Musashi took the wooden weapon in his hand and jumped into the shallow water. The sun's warmth spread across his back and arms, while his legs froze in the flowing water. A shiver went up his spine. He tightened his grip on his wooden sword and moved forward, oblivious to the cold, the battle, and the impending life-and-death struggle. Holding the carved sword directly in front of him, he saw Gan-ryu standing with his followers in the distance.

$$\mathcal{H}$$

The morning had grown bright. Gan-ryu paced furiously. His shouts carried down the beach. "I'm leaving. Musashi isn't coming. He has turned coward!" He started toward the boats, but his followers pleaded: "If Musashi should appear just after you leave, it would be you that people would call the coward. We must wait, at least for a while longer." And so they waited, looking westward toward the quiet village for a boat they didn't see arriving.

Just then, one of Gan-ryu's followers glanced over his shoulder. In the glow of the rising sun on the other end of the narrow island, a figure wrapped in watery mist waded toward them. "It's Musashi!" he yelled. Everyone turned toward the ghostly figure.

"He is still alive, yet already he looks like death," Gan-ryu said bitterly. He clutched his long sword. "You are late, Musashi," he yelled across the sand. "Coward! Forced to use delaying tactics. A cheap ploy. But my sword speaks louder than your childish antics." Gan-ryu thrust forward into the cold water.

Musashi advanced, his eyes like burning coals. The two were face to face. "You've lost, Gan-ryu," Musashi said calmly.

They jockeyed for position, maneuvering around each other, both searching for the advantage. Their footsteps were as smooth as if they were walking on clouds. Their minds were focused on their movements. It was as if there were no distinction between one man's movements and those of the other. Their training was so embedded in their being that action and reaction were completely spontaneous. All conscious thought had vanished. Two phantoms were at play at the water's edge in a deadly game of swords, one of them made of steel and one of them made of wood.

Gan-ryu advanced, immediately taking the initiative, as he always did. He carried his long, long sword high above his head, searching for a moment of weakness, sudden fear, and distraction in his opponent. Musashi, however, did not retreat. Unlike all the others, Musashi stepped forward, unafraid of his towering opponent. Gan-ryu was surprised to find himself instinctively backing up. Musashi advanced again, thrusting his sword in front of him. He looked like a cat ready to rip the eyes out of Gan-ryu's head with the swipe of its front claws.

And so they moved back and forth as the river lapped their feet. Suddenly, Gan-ryu's sword shot straight up and then down at Musashi's head. In a flash, Musashi dodged the blow, then leaped high into the air to avoid Gan-ryu's follow-up slash. In the split-second spark of swordplay, Gan-ryu's blade had come so close that it had sliced Musashi's headband, which went flying through the air. For a fleeting moment, Gan-ryu, blinded by the brilliant sun, smiled, thinking it was the head of Musashi that had gone flying. In the next instant, Musashi's wooden sword came crashing into Gan-ryu's skull.

It was over. Gan-ryu lay on the water's edge, still smiling.

He died believing he had won. Musashi looked past Gan-ryu at a single white cloud over the water's edge. Suddenly he was no longer the sun and the water, but Musashi Miyamoto once again. He felt the pain in his legs from the jump, and the gash on his forehead where Gan-ryu had torn off his headband. He knew that if it had been the width of one hair closer, he would be lying in the water now instead of Gan-ryu.

"What a man!" he said, as everyone gawked at the fallen body of the great swordsman.

"He was great, but you were greater," replied one of Gan-ryu's students, giving Musashi his due.

"No!" yelled Musashi. "Gan-ryu was the greatest swordsman. I have never seen anyone so strong, so fast as he was. He was magnificent!"

"I don't understand," replied the puzzled student. "If he was so strong, how did you defeat him?"

Musashi considered the question, still stunned to be alive. "Gan-ryu carried the sword of strength and skill, while I carried the sword of spirit and strategy. That was the only difference between us."

♓

Musashi and the boatman were silent as the boat plowed through the sunlit waters.

If Gan-ryu had won, thought the boatman, *I have no doubt he would be in the village getting drunk with his friends and admirers. He would be celebrating the killing. But not Musashi. He is a swordsman who truly values human life.*

The boatman turned to Musashi. "I am glad that you are alive. You scared me before when you spoke of my returning with your body. I had more confidence than you. I knew in my heart that you would win. I just didn't know how."

"I didn't either. I was just appreciating every moment. Would you like to hear a story?"

"From you? Definitely!"

THE LAST STRAWBERRY

Existence is but a dream within a dream.
Human life lasts but an instant.
We should spend it doing what is pleasant,
Enjoying every minute,
Never losing a moment's essence,
Or the beauty of a single sun that
sets before our eyes,
Never wasting the experience of
even a single delicious strawberry

– Meditation upon the poetry of the *Hagakure*

On a clear spring day, a young man was walking across a mountain meadow when he met a tiger. He turned on his heel and ran from the tiger as fast as he could, until he came to a precipice. In deep trouble, he grabbed the root of a wild vine and swung himself down over the edge. The tiger roared in anger above him, sniffing the air in wild anticipation of the delicious meal that seemed to be falling away. The tiger considered trying the vine itself, but decided against it.

Climbing down the vine toward the valley, the man saw a black bear hidden in the bush below him. The bear rose on its hind legs and swiped at the man dangling above it. It smacked its lips at the thought of a human dinner. The man scurried back up the rope. There the tiger waited.

"Of all the luck," the young man thought, "I have to encounter a *patient* tiger." So he stayed put, midway between the valley and the meadow, trying to decide if it was better to be eaten by a patient tiger or a flailing bear. He thought he would wait until either the bear or the tiger tired or found a better meal.

Hanging between the two, the young man suddenly noticed that two mice, one white and one black, had begun nibbling at the vine. He realized that death could not be avoided. Seeing a luscious strawberry growing out of the cliff side, the young man reached out and plucked it. How delicious it tasted! In his whole life, he had never eaten anything so grand.

None of us knows how long we have to live. It might be eighty years, it might be a day. The samurai prepares for death each day, living each day as if it were his last. And if it is not? He has given each moment of his life special meaning. If he should die tomorrow, he has lived today! And so goes each day of his life – each day that he has made special – of his own power, of his own will.

Some people mistakenly think that samurai knew only how to fight. The authentic samurai understood that the real fight was within – not to learn to kill, but to learn to live.

Musashi's Program for the Individual Warrior
After his duel with Gan-ryu, Musashi devoted more of his time to his writings and the development of his ideas, particularly on the nature of strategy. He wrote an outline for a sort of training program, a program to train the mind and the spirit:

1. Think of what is right and true.
2. Put the science into practice.
3. Become acquainted with the arts.
4. Become acquainted with the crafts.
5. Understand the negative and positive qualities in everything.
6. Learn to see everything accurately.
7. Become aware of what is not obvious.
8. Be careful even in small matters.
9. Don't do anything useless!

IV
Fighting the Shark

—✳—

A ship in a harbor is safe,
but that is not what ships are built for.

– Anonymous

A DREAM OF SHARKS

From the shore, I saw the gray fins splashing in the surf. The beach was closed for the third time that week. That meant another day of standing around instead of swimming. I was fourteen and not very patient. I loved swimming. I craved it. And the sharks were forcing me out of the water once again. I would spend yet another day walking along the boardwalk, waiting for the sharks to swim back out to sea.

Generally I felt really lucky living near the ocean. My summers were spent swimming. And in the cold, damp winters, I would go to the beach after school and walk for hours along the shore. I loved the salt smell, the wet air, the sea gulls, the hoarse sounds of the waves, the touch of the cool sand on my bare feet, the white clouds on the dark water, the horizon that always made me pensive – where does the world end and empty space begin? Nowhere else could nature replicate the glorious ocean sunsets. I loved the beach's solitude in winter and the excitement of the hordes of people in summer. I loved the playland where I worked each summer, getting paid to serve (and eat) hamburgers and cotton candy, and flirt with the girls.

I hated the sharks. I hated them for ruining my days of swimming. I hated their sleek movements and slimy features, their eyes, which appeared not to see yet let them know exactly where to go. And I hated the fact that they could devour me if they one day surprised me in the water.

I knew they were there even on days when they were not seen. They were always there. Sometimes we recognized it, and other times we pretended that the water was safe. The ocean is never safe; there are always dangers. But when you love ocean swimming enough, you take your chances and pretend you're brave.

My friends and I never talked about it, because that would mean having to admit to our deepest fears. But some nights there would be dreams. I would be happily swimming along, when all of a sudden a shark would appear out of the blue, open its mouth, and come right at me. In my dream, I could count its teeth, see into the depths of its throat. I would wake up in a cold sweat. Even after I left home to go to university, where the only swimming I did was in pools, every so often I would wake up in a cold sweat after another shark attack hundreds of miles from the ocean.

The dreams have never entirely stopped. But they did change radically. I was seventeen when I received my blue belt. A few nights later, I had the shark dream for the first time in a long time. But this time, instead of snapping awake when the shark approached, I jumped up and executed a powerful punch right to the tip of its sensitive nose. The shark glided to the side and disappeared into the dark ocean depths. I continued my swim.

$$\text{\Pisces}$$

I guess this is why I so love the martial arts. And it's funny, because it has nothing to do with real sharks. I have never been attacked by a shark, nor do I ever intend to be. Martial arts are really about conquering our deepest fears – in my case my subconscious fear of sharks. Fighting sharks or dragons, unfairness or cruelty – all battles we face are won or lost within ourselves, where we hold the knowledge of whether or not we can act with courage.

Before Musashi could defeat Gan-ryu, he had to conquer his own fear. To an experienced samurai such as he was, technique is always secondary to the mental state. I guess we could say that what we call the samurai spirit literally transforms the individual from the inside out. We dream different dreams than we once did.

Samurai Could Be Born or Made
Japanese society was made up of many rigid classes or levels. Originally based on what a person did – the nobility ruled, the samurai were warriors, peasants farmed and fished – these classes were held by families. Although many people were born into the samurai class, some warriors earned the high position of samurai by their merit on the battlefield. And someone born a samurai could also hold other positions, such as administrators in government, or even doctors.

THE SAMURAI DOCTOR

To see what is right and not do it is want of courage.

– Confucius

Several hundred years ago, there was a samurai who had studied medicine. He set up a clinic in a poor area of Japan and worked tirelessly to help his patients. He badly needed the help of an assistant, but had trouble keeping one. Every helper referred to him by his many doctor friends would quickly lose heart and leave in frustration over the futility of the work: so many sick people amongst the poor, so few doctors willing to give help; so much ignorance, so little pay!

At long last the samurai doctor was sent an apprentice who seemed tougher than most. One day, the doctor and his young assistant set out to make calls in one of the poorest parts of the city. Their first patient, an elderly woman, told them a sad story about a child who lived in an even worse district of the city, where the samurai doctor himself had never dared venture. The girl's father had died, and her mother, in terrible poverty, had married a man who drank himself into ruin. They were living more like animals than people. The old woman said that the man was terribly abusive to the girl, who was a virtual prisoner to her stepfather, and now she was taken seriously ill. There was no chance, the old woman said, that the stepfather would spend the money on a doctor for her. And without medical attention, she would surely die.

Upon hearing this story, the samurai doctor and his assistant went directly to the home of the girl, a shack that looked like it would collapse if you even looked at it too long. The samurai went in to examine the girl. Only the mother was home with her. The father was out drinking. The doctor saw that the child had been beaten. "This is no place for a child!" said the doctor. "I must take her to my clinic." The mother begged him to hurry and take her child before her husband returned with his friends.

The two doctors hurried out with the child only to confront, outside the house, the father with a gang of his drunken friends. The samurai doctor hadn't fought in years. Yet he could see no alternative to what lay before him. Dust and sand blew in the wind and into their eyes. The girl shielded her face, whether from her stepfather or from the blowing dirt, the doctor didn't know, but it was true that the men were not a pleasant sight – tough, drunk, and looking forward to a fight.

The man who had trained as a samurai in the shadow of one of Japan's great castles was now standing amid rabble who would no doubt, in a matter of seconds, attack him. If he wanted to take away his sick patient, he would have to fight. Or he could leave her there and go home. The first option was unpleasant, but the second was unimaginable.

Reluctantly, the samurai doctor put the girl down on the ground and went into the street to face his attackers. His assistant looked on in disbelief. How would they survive? They carried no swords with them, only medicine bags.

The rough men prepared for battle, happy in their numbers, circling like vultures around a wounded prey, ready to punish the doctor for daring to trespass into their territory.

"Let us pass," said the samurai doctor.

They scowled in response.

"In that case, I will do my best not to injure you," he said calmly.

The men laughed. "Can you not count?" one of them asked. The others snorted. The vultures moved in, slowly closing the circle around the doctor. Shoulders relaxed, stomach muscles taut, the prey waited. His eyes intense, not looking at any one of them in particular, the samurai doctor seemed to see everywhere. He faced them, knowing he was drawing upon his deepest power, something honed from years of training. One by one they attacked, each one from a different direction.

The doctor blocked each blow using a different counter-attack. One by one he sent them flying – one with a dislo-cated elbow, the next with a dislocated shoulder, a third with his wrist out of joint, a fourth struck hard in the jaw and left powerless to utter any more threats. Those left standing backed away down the street.

The doctor went to each of his attackers in turn, and with firm hands set each joint back in place. Then he picked up the child and glanced over his shoulder at the silent men. No longer did they look menacing. They seemed puzzled. *What type of man would risk his life so boldly for a little girl?* As if the question in their minds was asked aloud, he replied, "She is human too."

The assistant emerged from behind a pillar. He had thought he would be carrying the samurai home in pieces. But they were all alive. How could just one samurai, without swords, do all this?

The samurai doctor looked at him and said, "It is up to samurai to do such things. That is why we work to have strength and courage."

"I am a samurai too," said the assistant. "I have also had training in the martial arts, but I have no such courage as you. I have never seen anything like this, and you did it without swords."

"The sword is only the symbol of the samurai," the samurai doctor replied. "It is what we carry in our hearts that truly makes us samurai. I believe that, at first, you looked down on my work with the poor. I hope you will consider staying. It is here that you will learn to be a real samurai."

The young assistant had decided to stay the moment he had seen the attackers flying through the courtyard. *This is a samurai who will change the world, and being around him will change me*, he thought. He knew that the spirit of the samurai doctor was contagious, and that this was something he truly wanted to catch.

The young samurai had learned more than medicine from the master. He learned about the meaning of pride. He had always been a proud samurai, defining himself as a warrior from an important family, and seeing a difference between himself and the people he worked with. He felt they were beneath him. The actions of his master made him see that his pride was actually vanity, and his honor was misplaced. The samurai doctor took pride in what he did, not what he was. His pride was in his actions that always contributed to the lives of others.

FREEDOM FROM FEAR

If we cannot conquer our personal fears,
then a life of a thousand years is a tragedy.
If we can conquer them,
then a life of a single day is a triumph.

– Bruce Lee

The shogun was the supreme military ruler of Japan. In his employ was a samurai who had a daughter, Ohashi. As befitted a samurai's daughter, she had received an excellent education in literature and the arts. She was admired by everyone and beloved by her father and three brothers.

Also in the shogun's court was a rich official, a man who was coarse and mean. He had outlived two wives, and had begun remarking on Ohashi's beauty, her sweetness, her charm. Ohashi's father had felt disgusted at hearing the words from such a cruel man, so unworthy of his lovely daughter.

But fate is unfair. Hard times came. Ohashi's father lost his position in court and his family was thrown into poverty. He saw no choice but to sell his beautiful Ohashi in marriage to the official.

So Ohashi became the wife of a government official who was famous not for his competence or his compassion, but for his bad temper and arrogance. Everyone despised him as much as they admired his young wife. And he was cruel to Ohashi. When she did not do exactly what he liked, he would beat her. She knew that he continued seeing other women, shaming her at the same time she welcomed his absence.

Her husband blamed her for any detail that displeased him: the bed wasn't comfortable; the rice wine wasn't the right temperature; her opinions were always wrong. When she spoke up, he called her stupid. When she said nothing, he yelled at her for never having an opinion. Ohashi was torn between her past joy and her present sorrow, between her high ideals as a samurai woman and her fallen state with a man she detested. She felt like killing herself so she wouldn't have to bring children into such a sad life. From the moment she woke, she feared each day. She jumped at noises. She became terrified of thunder. She became scared of the dark.

One day a samurai came to the castle to conduct government business with Ohashi's husband. The stranger held himself in a proud and dignified manner, and had piercing eyes. He was a man of education and culture. He met Ohashi in the courtyard outside the house. She bowed respectfully to him, as he was a high-ranking samurai, and he surprised her by returning a bow as deep and respectful as hers. A few days later, she met him again as he was leaving from a meeting with her husband.

"Good morning," he said respectfully, and bowed with the same deference he had shown her before. "You are Ohashi, and I am honored to meet you."

"How do you know who I am?" Ohashi asked.

"Because you are famous for your beauty and your charm." He paused for a moment. "And for being the unfortunate wife of the shogun's official."

"How do you know about that?" she asked.

"Many people know that your husband is a cruel man. And I knew your father. In times of peace, many samurai lose their positions, even great samurai. We all feel for your father, and it pains me deeply to know your situation." His eyes were as gentle as they were powerful.

"You cannot imagine what it is to be married to a man like my husband, to have to live in the same house with his cruelty and temper, to have to sleep in the same bed with him each night. That is, of course, when he is not out with his other women."

"If I had a wife such as you, I would never look at another woman, never even think of another woman, much less be with someone else."

"Why are you not married?"

"I am still waiting. The shogun wants me to be one of his personal retainers. He will choose a wife for me. I cannot marry until he arranges it. And I may be an old man by the time he gets around to it. Maybe he wants me to concentrate only on martial arts.

"Of course," he continued, "my problems are nothing compared to yours. Fate sometimes plays strange tricks on human beings. If I had enough money, I would buy you out of this loveless home and give you back to your father, but I don't have enough money. I do have ways that could help you, only you must put your faith in me. Let me tell you a story."

The samurai cleared his throat and began: "I had a friend who was killed in an ambush right before my eyes. He lunged in front of an arrow that was meant for me. His wife and children were inconsolable. His wife eventually married another man, who seemed gentle at first, but eventually treated her badly, beating her and the children and threatening to kill them if they should run away."

"How horrible," said Ohashi, glad that she had no children for her husband to terrorize.

"But what counts is that while my friend lived, his family had a happiness that was truly beautiful. He and his wife created beautiful children. And they all lived a wonderful life together. As it says in the *Hagakure*, life is but a dream within a dream. One morning they woke up and it was over – all that they had created and had labored so hard to develop.

"You see, your father's fate is not so bad. At least he is still alive. Although he is poor, he still has his family. And I am sure that he still has hopes for you, however difficult your situation. I am certain that he dreams that you will somehow find contentment, however difficult that may be. I say that with confidence because I know you come from a samurai family and you understand how a great samurai dedicates his life to facing challenges.

"Remember who you are and find strength in that. You must tell yourself that you will never give up. Never lose hope. Find beauty in the little things around you and they will sustain you. You will find that this will be your escape from the realm of misery."

Taking seriously the words of the samurai, Ohashi began to practice what he had suggested. Every breath of fresh air, every flower that she saw, every sunset, became a source of happiness to her. She discovered that the world was full of little joys all around her.

One day in a storm, with thunder rolling and lightning striking all around her, she was surprised to discover that she was unafraid. She had found joy in the thunderstorm. She did not have to be afraid. She found further strength everyday in her simple capacity to smile.

The years passed. One night Ohashi's husband died in his sleep. The shogun summoned Ohashi to the castle. Others warned her of more tragedy to follow. "The shogun will probably give you away to an older man to marry now that you are 'used goods.'" Sure enough, when she arrived, she was informed that the shogun had arranged a new marriage for her. She was sent to the adjoining room to meet her new husband.

Much to her surprise, it was the kind samurai she had met years earlier, whose words she had never forgotten. He looked much older. A horrible scar marred the left side of his face. He greeted her warmly.

"The shogun has finally arranged my marriage. Will you have me as your husband?"

Even with the scar, he had the same good humor and kind character. "The shogun has made the decision. It is not for me to decide," she replied seriously. Then she laughed. "It is my choice also!"

The samurai explained that his scar was a price he paid as a samurai. It was a duel he had to accept, although he hated being placed in such a situation. At least he was still alive, and he had won the fight! "The man who lost," he noted, "was in far worse shape." She laughed again, and realized that she had loved him from their first meeting years ago. She understood that she loved him even more now. She saw how he had suffered, but could still smile, just as he had taught her to do.

The samurai said, "If you can smile through the life you have had, you will be able to find happiness even with a man as ugly as I. If you will marry me, I will do everything to make you happy."

"Yes," she replied. She looked closely at his face and realized that the scar was a mark of how he had not given up. It truly showed how beautiful his spirit was. And so they married, and each took it as their task to build the happiness of the other.

Ohashi learned to never give up. This is one of the most important lessons a samurai can learn. Even when life seemed unbearable, Ohashi focused on the small beauties all around her, and developed the strength to persevere. When her situation finally changed for the better, she went forward with optimism instead of bitterness. Even in adversity, a samurai looks for ways to become stronger, instead of excuses for being weaker.

HOW TO DEFEAT THREE SAMURAI WITH TWO CHOPSTICKS

Intensely enjoying his simple meal, a samurai sat at an inn with a bowl of broth and noodles, his superb swords at his side. Three rogue samurai entered the inn and saw the man's magnificent weapons. How they wanted the beautiful swords!

They were confident that the man would be no match for the three of them. They jeered and jostled him, trying to provoke a fight. They did not succeed. The samurai continued eating, as oblivious to their taunts as he was to the three flies that buzzed around him in the warm air of the inn.

Finally, when all the diners in the inn were sure that the men were about to draw their swords, the lone samurai calmly pushed away his bowl and took up his chopsticks. With a flick of his fingers, he captured one of the three flies. He threw the fly in his empty rice bowl, lifted his chopsticks again, and in short order clipped the second fly between his chopsticks and threw it in the bowl beside the first. As the three samurai stood watching in astonishment, he reached over his left shoulder with the chopsticks and trapped the third fly, tossing it to join the two already in the bowl.

The three rogue samurai grabbed their things and ran for the door. It was only later that they found out that the man with whom they had tried to pick a fight was Musashi Miyamoto. They realized that they could have been thrust out the door as easily as the flies were plunged into the rice bowl.

Even for a well-trained samurai, three attacking swordsmen is a formidable challenge. Musashi knew he could have cut them down easily, but doing so would not be what reflects the excellence of a samurai. Rather it is his complete and total control of the situation. Musashi had so much self-confidence that one can readily imagine a whole army coming in, and he would still act in the same detached manner, scaring them off with the play of chopsticks.

SAMURAI IN A SIDESTREET

One summer as a university student, I was visiting the Middle East, carrying only a small backpack containing some clothes, a bathing suit, my books, and my brown belt. Traveling through Turkey, Iran, and Afghanistan, I had been warned that I was going through some dangerous areas. But since I carried only my backpack and was dressed as a student, I didn't feel I would attract attention as someone worth robbing. I was vigilant, nevertheless, and while eating lunch one day in a small town, I had a bad feeling about a table of men laughing at me while I ate. I decided to leave my lunch and get out.

Paying my bill, I observed that the group of three men laughing at me had grown to seven. That was okay; I was on my way out anyway. As I quickly exited, however, the seven of them got up and followed me outside. I moved rapidly toward the train station, four blocks away. When I glanced behind me, there were more men – about eleven – but I was no longer counting.

I had no doubt about their intentions. I quickly turned the corner into a little sidestreet where there was a bunch of large garbage cans lined up. I quickly removed my backpack and placed it on the ground, and then crouched down behind one of the cans. I heard the men round the corner into the sidestreet. They were talking excitedly. I could tell that they were looking forward to what was about to happen. I knew from the tone of their voices that they were asking each other where I had gone.

Suddenly I leaped out in front of them with a loud *kiai*, which almost gave a heart attack to the man standing right in front of me. He instinctively jumped back, smashing furiously into the man behind him, who in turn fell hard into the man behind him, and so on. I felt as if I had unexpectedly hit the jackpot in a bowling alley, witnessing a chain reaction of exploding pins in the dust of this back alley. Standing in a fighting karate stance with my open hands held high, I watched them disappear into the haze of dust, as they all fell upon one another trying to escape. In moments, I was alone on the street wondering what had happened.

After it was all over, I still had trouble believing it had actually occurred. Yet there I was, still in the smelly alleyway with my backpack on the ground beside me. I picked it up and continued my walk to the train station.

♓

It wasn't that I had learned how to fight. I didn't lift a finger. Yet I knew the samurai spirit had become an integral part of me. Inside my head lived the spirit of Musashi Miyamoto and the Samurai Doctor, and they permeated my being. I was really proud to be who I was, and knew that feeling would stay with me my whole life.

What began as one of the most frightening episodes of my life ended as one of the funniest. I had anticipated a Samurai Doctor conclusion but, much to my surprise, it was a Musashi finish – without the chopsticks.

As a teacher, I see people alter their lives through martial arts. The self-defence they learn is important, but they are doing something far more profound – learning to confront their deepest fears. In every class, we have people attacking us from all sides with all their might. What often seems frightening at first, in time loses its sting. We become confident in our powers, knowing that we can easily defend ourselves – every night in the training hall – just as Musashi did with his chopsticks or the Samurai Doctor did against all those attackers.

THE MASTER SWORDSMAN
WHO NEVER HELD A SWORD

*The true mastery of an art is not
the development of technique,
but the mastery of self.*

– Martial arts adage

Yagyu Tajima no Kami Munenori was a great swordsman and teacher to the shogun Tokugawa Iyemitsu. One day, a personal guard of the shogun came to Tajima wishing to take lessons in swordplay. The master looked at the young man before him and replied, "As I observe, you seem to be a master of the art yourself. Please tell me with whom you have previously studied, before you take me on as a new teacher."

The guardsman replied, "I am ashamed to tell you that I have never before learned the art of swordplay."

"Do you think that you can fool me?" Tajima asked sternly. "I am teacher to the shogun himself. Do you think that I cannot tell an expert swordsman who stands right in front of my eyes? My judgment on such matters never fails!"

"Sir, I do not mean to disagree, but I really know nothing."

Tajima looked at the young man carefully, with eyes that seemed to penetrate right into his very soul. He thought a long time before speaking again. "If you say so, then it must be. Yet I am still sure of your being a master of something, though I do not know what."

"Sir, if you insist, I will tell you something that might be pertinent. When I was still a boy, I was afraid of many things. Perhaps I was no different than many other boys in that. I don't know. But the thought came to me one day that if I truly wish to be a great samurai, then I ought not be afraid. I must conquer my fears! I set upon this challenge every day of my life. I have grappled with this problem now for many years, and then one day I realized that the issue had entirely ceased to bother me. I had mastered my fears! Perhaps this is what you are seeing?"

"Exactly!" exclaimed Tajima. "It is what I meant. I am relieved that I made no mistake in my judgment of you. I knew you were not a liar, yet there was something about you that was more than meets the eye. The ultimate secret of swordsmanship lies in being released from the fear of death. I have trained hundreds of pupils, but so far none of them really deserves the final certificate for swordsmanship. You need no technical training. You are already a master!"

We all have secret fears. Conquering these fears is at the heart of the samurai spirit. It is also at the heart of the samurai ethical tradition. Only a person secure within himself is capable of helping others. Someone insecure, afraid, and whiny cannot confront real danger and prevail. What counts is not technique, but the spirit of the person. What Tajima most sought to develop in his students was a spirit that could never be defeated. Samurai training forced each student to reach deeply within himself and shape up.

V

Sharks with Human Faces

—✳—

An ordinary man, if he feels that he has been ridiculed,
will draw his sword and risk his very life,
but he will not be called a courageous man for doing so.
A superior man is never alarmed,
even in the most unexpected situations,
because he has a great soul and a noble objective.

– Gishin Funakoshi,
one of the Okinawan founders of modern karate

THE SWORD OF LIFE AND THE SWORD OF DEATH

A samurai warrior was crossing a wooden bridge over a creek in the forest, and saw coming toward him a Buddhist monk. Knowing the reputation monks have for education and wisdom, he decided to ask a question that had always troubled him.

"Excuse me, sir," he began. "Could you be so kind as to tell me whether heaven and hell really exist?"

The monk looked at him intensely and, all of a sudden, his eyes turned to fire as he yelled, "You are an ignorant samurai! Do you think that I would waste my time trying to explain something so complex to someone as stupid as you?"

Enraged, the warrior drew his sword, intending to strike down the offending monk for insulting him. *Doesn't he know any better than that?* the samurai asked himself as he raised his sword over his head.

As he did, the monk exclaimed, "Here open the gates of hell!" gesturing at the drawn sword.

Surprised, the samurai stopped, pondered a moment, and then slowly resheathed his sword.

"Here open the gates of heaven!" observed the monk.

The sword, the hand – what matters is what one does with it, and as the monk implied, the choices are of our own creation.

THE ART OF DEFEATING
THE ENEMY WITHOUT HANDS

To win one hundred victories in one hundred battles
is not the highest skill.
To subdue the enemy without fighting
is the highest skill.

– Sun Tzu

It was a hot summer day. Noguchi was in a very bad mood, which was not so extraordinary for Noguchi but that day was particularly bad. The ferry across the channel was very crowded, and Noguchi, a samurai, did not like mingling with common people. They smelled bad. They spoke too loudly, and they had an annoying tendency to always be in his way. On board the boat, every way he turned, there was one of them before him – a smelly man, or a woman with a crying baby.

Noguchi could not understand why anyone would want a baby anyway. He was above such things. He didn't waste his time with women and children. He practiced martial arts all day, and he enjoyed being in situations where he could use his skills. That was the one redeeming feature about being on a stupid boat with crowds of people. Someone was bound to do something that would require Noguchi to make some "correction." And that invariably involved swordplay, which was his passion.

He took out a flask of rice wine and started drinking. In no time at all, he was drunk. Oh, how he loved that feeling! He fumbled in his pocket for his pipe and began filling it. A crowd of people gathered around the tipsy samurai. He bragged about what a great warrior he was and about all the men he had defeated. Noguchi's audience noted that he looked too young for all the experience he claimed to have, but he was certainly very muscular.

The boat suddenly swayed and Noguchi banged into the railing, dropping his pipe into the water. His face turned scarlet. People backed away, wary of his anger. Noguchi swore and reached for his sword.

An older man approached respectfully, dropped on his knees and offered Noguchi his pipe. "Please sir, take mine," he said.

Noguchi looked at the man with eyes of fury. "Old man, do you really think I would ever put something of yours in my mouth? I am a samurai!" He slowly drew out his sword, relishing every moment as the crowd watched in horror. The old man lay before Noguchi, his head touching the deck in a deep bow. He shivered uncontrollably as the samurai admired how his shining sword glistened in the sunlight.

"Look," a boy yelled, breaking the tension. "There's another samurai!" He pointed to the other end of the boat, where a man with white hair sat. His eyes were closed, but he seemed alert, listening carefully to what was going on.

Everyone ran over to see this second samurai, even Noguchi, who was curious and a bit annoyed that a samurai had been secretly observing him. *Who the heck is he?* Noguchi was thinking. *What makes him think he can steal my thunder? And just at the best part!*

Noguchi walked through the throng, reached over, and shook the smaller man. "You also carry a pair of swords. Why not say something?"

"The sea rocks this boat enough! Why don't you leave everyone in peace so we can enjoy the refreshing sea breezes and the sparkle of the sun. It's much cooler out here on the ocean. Even a hothead like you can learn to appreciate that, if you try." The white-haired man's calm inspired the others, who felt less afraid in his presence. Sensing this, Noguchi dramatically pulled out his sword to the gasps of the onlookers.

The old man slowly rose, carefully picking straw from his kimono. "My art is different from yours. It consists not in defeating others, but in not being defeated."

This incensed Noguchi even more. "You carry the swords of the samurai, old man. Have you no longer the might of the samurai?"

"I need neither swords nor might to defeat you. But let us not trouble these good people with our quarrel." The older samurai pointed across to the deeper water, far out to sea. "There, on one of the deserted islands, the greater samurai will prevail."

"And you will fight me without swords?"

"Certainly."

"What is your school of swordsmanship, then?"

"It is known as the School of Defeating the Enemy Without Hands; that is, without using a sword."

"Why, then, do you carry a sword?"

"This sword is not meant to kill others, but is a tool of my own development. It represents the search within myself to cut out fear, selfishness, and indecision. This sword symbolizes the power of my quest. It tells me I can never quit. It demands of me that I never be defeated in the things I wish to do."

"Fine, you'll fight me without swords! Let's go!" Noguchi called for the boatman. "I'm anxious to have a go at this old man who will fight me without swords," he said. "I hope I won't become too afraid when we arrive at the island! You're not going to spook me, are you, old man?"

The boat advanced toward a solitary island far off in the blue sea. Noguchi pranced with excitement as they neared the island, so keen was he to prove once again how great he was. As they approached, Noguchi jumped off the boat and, drawing his sword, stood standing on the water's edge ready for combat. The older samurai removed his own swords and gave them to the boatman.

"So you still think you can defeat me without swords, old man," Noguchi shouted.

"You raise your sword without understanding, Noguchi, so even the boatman's bamboo pole can conquer you." The old man grabbed the pole and, with one great shove, he pushed the ship back out to sea, safely out of reach of the man with a sword on the shore.

"Coward!" Noguchi yelled over the sound of the waves. "What do you think you are doing? Come out and fight!"

"I *have* fought." Noguchi heard the old man's voice call over the wind. "And, without a sword, I have defeated you.

Wits are the best weapon of all. This is my No-hands school."
The boat continued on its journey, minus one passenger.

> ### *Thieves in Old Japan*
> In any society, a thief is a thief. But in Japan, a society that
> so values honor, thieves are particularly looked down on.
> Many samurai stories take place at a time in Japanese
> history when thieves were as innumerable as grains of sand
> on a beach. In these stories, the thief is the complete
> opposite of the samurai. Deceit and theft are the opposite
> of the honor and respect of the samurai spirit. A thief
> brings disgrace not only on himself, but on his entire
> family. Even after a thief was executed, his body received
> no respect, but was used by samurai to test the sharpness
> of their swords and the power of their strokes.

THE KIDNAPPED CHILD

A thief, chased by a band of villagers, had taken a young boy
hostage. Threatening to slit the throat of his prisoner if
anyone came near, he sat with the boy in a barn while the villagers waited anxiously a short distance away. When the boy's
mother approached in tears, the thief became nervous. She
fell back, terrified for her child's life. The kidnapper became

more and more agitated as other, calmer people tried to reason with him. He made no demands. He just sat with his knife to the throat of the child. Everyone feared the worst, but couldn't think of anything to do without endangering the boy.

A traveling samurai entered what appeared to be an abandoned village. Then, in the distance, he saw a crowd of people and heard a woman wailing. He approached and asked what was happening. People saw a sign of hope in his arrival, but what could he do? As soon as he tried to get close, the thief would become agitated and perhaps murder the child.

The samurai, an admirer of the teachings of Musashi Miyamoto, sat down to think things out. Musashi had always stressed the importance of developing a strategy and approaching a problem with an intelligent and resolute mind. What would Musashi do in a situation like this?

Suddenly the warrior jumped up. He asked his hosts to get him a pail of hot water and a razor. It seemed a strange time for a shave, but they were sure he must have an idea. When the implements arrived, he asked their help in cutting off his spectacular hair. They watched in horror as he shaved his head and began to resemble a Buddhist priest. Somebody found a priest's robe and, removing his swords and elegant clothing, the samurai put on the plain, rough garment.

It was amazing how his demeanor changed, from that of a fierce warrior to that of a gentle priest. The villagers were aware of the great sacrifice he had just made. His swords and clothes could be put on again later, but what of his hair, which a samurai always kept long and tied in a distinguished style?

The samurai himself was undisturbed by these thoughts. He asked the boy's mother to bring him some rice cakes.

Carrying the cakes on a large plate, he approached the barn, gently explaining that he was a Buddhist priest here to offer some rice cakes for the thief and his hostage to eat. "You need some nourishment. And the boy must eat as well. I am here to bring you some food, and then I will immediately turn around and go back."

The kidnapper let him approach a little closer and then cried out: "Stop! That is close enough." After eyeing the "priest" carefully, the kidnapper reached for a rice cake. "I can't reach," he said as he tried to keep his grip on the boy while reaching to take the cakes. "But you can't come any closer!"

The samurai threw the kidnapper one of the rice cakes. The man easily caught it in his hand, still holding the boy. The samurai threw him the second cake – this time a little to the side. The kidnapper reached to grab the rice cake, and in a flash the samurai leaped into the barn. The villagers heard the sound of a fierce struggle. Finally, the kidnapper walked out of the barn alone, looking stunned. What had happened inside that barn? People were afraid to imagine. A moment later, the kidnapper crumpled to the ground.

The samurai emerged from the barn with the frightened boy in his arms. As the crowd of onlookers cried out in joy, he reunited the boy and his mother. Mother and son returned home. The samurai changed back into his regular clothes, stashed his swords in his belt, and continued on his journey.

As evening fell, his shaved head became cold. He missed his thick hair. But he was happy to be a samurai, and thankful for the gift that his training had given him. He knew Musashi would be proud! He had maintained a calm mind and had faced, unarmed, a man brandishing a knife.

HAKAMADARE THE THIEF

An enemy you vanquish remains your enemy.
An enemy you convince becomes your friend.

– Chinese proverb

A thousand years ago, Hakamadare was the most renowned thief in Japan. His methods were simple. He was muscular and imposing, and he was unafraid to fight if he had to. Usually he didn't have to. He would select a victim, follow him, and, when the moment was right, ask his victim for his clothes or food or whatever else he wanted. People were afraid of him and were quick to meet his demands so that they could carry on in good health.

Hakamadare saw little need to work as hard as everyone else. It was easier for him to "ask" others when he needed something. And he didn't have to waste his time in the market. He simply picked out the best that other people had spent time and effort selecting. He wore the richest clothes and ate the finest foods. He knew that he had a comfortable life and he appreciated his good fate.

Autumn was approaching. The leaves were falling and the weather was becoming colder. Hakamadare realized that his summer clothes were no longer adequate. It occurred to him that it was time for him to do some "shopping." But the hour

74

was late. That the market place was dark and empty did not trouble him. What did bother him was that it was unlikely that he would encounter anyone on the streets until morning. He would have to spend a cold night in his thin clothes. He should have thought of this earlier. Oh well, it was just a question of waiting a few hours until daylight. Then the streets would be teeming with victims.

As he was about to curl up in a doorway to sleep, he saw a man walking down the street. The man appeared to be holding something in his hand that he brought to his mouth. Judging by the sound Hakamadare was hearing, the man was holding a flute.

Hakamadare could not believe his good fortune. He looked around. The man was well dressed and was unaccompanied by any bodyguards. He was totally caught up in the music he was playing. He seemed oblivious to everything – to the houses around him, to the hour, and to the fact that a man of his wealth should not be strolling in the street unprotected. *This will be too easy*, thought Hakamadare. Just for the sport, he decided to follow the man before moving into action.

At first, Hakamadare enjoyed the fun of stalking a foolish person, and the anticipation of stealing a large purse. But as he followed, he realized that there was something strange about his quarry's conduct. Although Hakamadare was making plenty of noise (that was part of the fun!) and the man must have known that someone was stalking him, he didn't seem in the least bit worried. He never stopped playing the flute, even for a moment, as if the minor disturbance of being stalked was not going to ruin his harmony with the night and the music.

Hakamadare ran in front of the man. The flute player glanced at him but did not change his pace. Hakamadare ran round and round him, with the same result. The man simply raised his eyes to look, and continued making his beautiful music. It wasn't possible to jump on him, as Hakamadare would usually do. The man was unafraid. This made Hakamadare nervous. He backed off.

Hakamadare the Thief was suddenly overcome with fear – fear of this eccentric, obviously well-to-do man who was completely unperturbed by the imposing stranger following him in the dark of night on a deserted street. For the first time in his life, it was Hakamadare, not his intended victim, who was shaking right down to his bones. *What is happening? Why am I afraid?* he asked himself.

He had no answer. But he had great confidence in his martial abilities. It was cold and he was not about to give up the beautiful suit of clothes walking in front of him. *Take a chance!* he told himself.

Hakamadare drew his sword and, with a loud *kiai*, jumped in front of the flute player. The man, for the first time, put aside his flute and looked at the drawn sword. "May I ask what you think you are doing?" he asked.

Hakamadare was struck by an awesome fear, as if he had been addressed by a devil. He dropped on his hands and knees in a position of complete submission to this demon.

"What are you doing?" the man repeated.

"I am trying to rob you," Hakamadare blurted out.

"You are? Well, you are certainly going about it in a strange way. What is your name?"

"I am Hakamadare," he said proudly, but with a tremor in his voice.

"Yes, I have heard that name. A very dangerous fellow, I am told – brawny, very good with a sword." Then the man said, "Follow me," and continued playing the flute.

Hakamadare sheepishly followed the man as if pulled along by some invisible force. He felt that he could never escape from this man's power, no matter how he tried. They passed through a beautiful gate and crossed the sumptuous gardens surrounding a large house. Hakamadare realized that his intended victim must be an important official.

The man removed his shoes and entered the house. "Wait here," he said. A few moments later he came outside and handed Hakamadare a beautiful kimono made of heavy cotton – one that would keep him very warm indeed. "If in the future you need something, come and tell me. If you jump on somebody who doesn't know your intentions, you may get hurt."

Hearing these words, the thief realized he was in the presence of Governor Yasumasa, a famous warrior known for his strong mind and incredible power. His weapon – a flute – was stronger than any sword.

Later, when Hakamadare was eventually arrested and led past the governor's house on his way to prison, he said to his guards, "I know that man."

Nobody believed him.

To test the true mettle of a man, give him power. Yasumasa exemplifies the samurai ethic of developing strength, not to possess power over others, but to have power over yourself. For Yasumasa, the flute was his weapon, and his compassion was his strength.

I try to remember this story every time I get angry. I tell myself, *Be a real samurai. Keep control. Be gentle!* And so I've saved myself a lot of grief – grief that would have been purely self-inflicted.

The Art of Tea

In the Japan of earlier years, the teamaster was a highly respected artist. He specialized in the creation of a relaxing and harmonious environment, as well as in the art of brewing superb tea.

The teaman's room was decorated with exquisite harmony and simplicity, perhaps with a single painting or flower, all pleasing to the eye and to the soul. The teaman would bring the water to the proper temperature, creating a beautiful music from the sound of the liquid boiling, like a stream dancing through the forest. He carefully steeped the highest-quality tea for just the right amount of time. And the art of serving the tea was sublime – his hands not just holding, but caressing the cup, as he poured the steaming liquid with superb self-control.

The samurai, in the presence of a master teaman, was relieved of the tensions of his difficult profession. Even in the midst of the most formidable challenges and dangers, the samurai would find serenity in the calm presence of a master teaman.

THE TEAMASTER AND THE BRUISER

In the seventeenth century, Lord Yama-no-uchi wanted to take his teamaster along with him on his official visit to Edo (now Tokyo). The teamaster was not happy about this, for Edo was not a peaceful place, and he was not a samurai capable of defending himself. His intuition told him there would inevitably be trouble for him there.

Yet his master insisted. The lord obviously desired to show off the special talents of his teamaster to his colleagues in the big city. To counter the teaman's arguments, he gave him the attire of a samurai to wear, including two swords. He explained that no one would trouble him when he was "dressed to kill."

The teamaster's visit was indeed uneventful. He stayed at the host's house, performing the tea ceremony for the many samurai who came to experience his artistry. One day he was given time to go and sightsee in the famous city.

Dressed as a samurai, he set out to visit an ancient temple. He passed a rough-looking samurai leaning against a large rock. The samurai was obviously a ronin, a samurai who has lost his position, perhaps due to chance, personal disgrace, or incompetence. The teamaster did not want to walk past the masterless samurai, fearing that there might be trouble, and he hesitated. That hesitation was a mistake. The ruffian accosted him.

"I see from your crest that you are a samurai from Tosa and therefore a student of the famous Yama-no-uchi. I would consider it a great honor if you permitted me to try my skill in swordplay with you," the man said.

Now, even the teamaster recognized the ronin's request as a challenge to a duel to the death. He understood that his moment of hesitation had thrown him into hot water, and that he was well on the way to being cooked.

"I am not actually a samurai," replied the teamaster. "I am only dressed as one to please my master. I am a teamaster, and hardly worthy to be your opponent."

"Nevertheless, samurai or teamaster, you carry two swords. We will fight."

The ronin's real hope was that the teaman would offer him money to avoid the fight. Then he would be able to boast that he defeated a samurai from Tosa, a student of the great Yama-no-uchi. But the teamaster had no money and, realizing that there was no escape, he accepted his fate. He was ready to die under the ronin's sword.

Even though he wasn't a samurai, the teamaster did not wish to die dishonorably. He remembered that he had seen a swordsman's training school just a short distance away. Perhaps he could go and ask the master at least how to hold the sword. That way he could face his inevitable death standing up as a samurai for the last moments of his life.

"If you insist that we must fight, then I have no choice but to agree. But since I am on my master's business, I must first make my report to him. Then I will come back to meet you here. You must give me a bit of time."

The ronin agreed. The teamaster rushed to the school and

made an urgent request to see the master. The *sensei* was teaching a class, and his assistant was reluctant to disturb him for such a strange and unexpected entreaty. Yet there was something so extraordinary about this man before him that he went to get the master.

The master listened intently to the story of a man caught in the grip of fate, hurtling toward a disastrous finale. "I am not a samurai, but if I am so dressed and must fight, then I wish to die as a samurai! Will you please help me?" asked the teamaster.

The master was surprised. "Pupils come to study here to learn how to fight with the sword. They are seldom interested in learning how to face death well. But before I begin to teach you how to face death as a samurai, could you please honor me by serving me a cup of tea?"

The teamaster of Tosa was delighted to have a last chance to practice his beloved art. Forgetting about the impending tragedy, he proceeded to prepare tea with the utmost serenity. The master swordsman watched closely as the master of tea went through all the stages of the art as if it were the only business in the world that concerned him. The master swordsman felt humbled in the presence of someone with such a concentrated state of mind. At the end, he sat tranquilly, enjoying the aroma wafting from his delicious cup of tea, savoring the delectable taste within his mouth, experiencing the feel of the cup he held in his two hands, which seemed to warm his whole body.

"There you are!" exclaimed the swordmaster. "There is no need for you to learn the art of dying as a samurai. Your state of mind is more than enough to cope with any opponent.

"When you see your ronin, proceed as follows. First, imagine you are about to serve tea for a guest. Greet him cordially, apologize for the delay, and tell him that you are now ready. For you really are ready! Take off your outer coat, fold it up, and carefully place your fan on it, just as you do when you prepare your tea ceremony. Put on your headband, tie your sleeves, and adjust your samurai gown. You are now prepared. Draw your sword, and lift it high up above your head in full readiness to strike down your opponent. Focus your thoughts on your combat, as you would focus on making tea. When you hear him give a yell, strike him down with your sword. It will probably end in a draw as you slay each other, for his superior technique will give him no greater advantage than your superior state of mind."

The teaman thanked the master for teaching him how to be a samurai, if even for such a brief time. He would be able to die proudly without disgracing his lord.

He returned to his opponent, stood straight, and bowed. He scrupulously followed all the instructions of the swordmaster. He carried within him the same state of mind he had when he was serving tea. Narrowing his eyes, he slowly raised his sword high up above his head.

As he held his own sword firmly, the ronin saw before him an altogether different person from the man he had met in the road. His eyes moved quickly from his opponent's sword to his fiercely focused eyes, but he could see no opening in which to attack. The teaman appeared to him now as the very embodiment of fearlessness.

Instead of yelling and advancing upon his opponent, the ronin slowly retreated. Finally he cried out, "I'm finished."

Then he dropped his sword and fell to his knees in front of the teaman. He asked the teaman's pardon for his rudeness and begged to be spared. The teaman gave permission for the ronin to leave without harm.

The teaman placed his swords back in the sheaths, where he believed they had always belonged. He had lived a samurai experience instead of dying a samurai death.

It is unlikely that this is a true story. But this tale was a favorite of samurai, which shows us how important its message is. The teaman generally knows nothing about swordplay and cannot in any way be a match for a trained swordsman. The story succeeds, however, in giving us an idea of what a person can accomplish in a situation even without the "necessary" technical training, if only his mind is resolute. The only failure is not trying.

SAMURAI ON A BICYCLE

A few years ago, I was speeding down a wide Toronto street on my bicycle when I saw two people fighting on the sidewalk. A kid of about seventeen was being pushed and punched by a very large man. Seeing a bicycle lying on the ground next to the kid, I guessed that he must have been riding on the crowded sidewalk and had accidentally slammed into the man.

It was probably one too many careless bicyclists for the man to tolerate – I could sympathize with his reaching the breaking point. Yet I also felt companionship with the poor guy getting his head smashed in. After all, he was a fellow cyclist. He was also just a young man who had already paid for his mistake with his broken bicycle. I couldn't help feeling that this muscle-bound guy was punishing all teenagers for being in his way, taking out his aggression on one person for the trouble he thought that all teenagers caused him. Like many people, he probably blamed teenagers for the increase in crime, in violence, in welfare cases – for virtually all the troubles of the world. It was unfair.

I jumped off my bicycle and ran between the two, trying to calm down the red-faced man. Flexing his muscles to show he meant business, he yelled at me to get out of his way so that he could "teach this stupid kid a lesson about riding his bike on the sidewalk." But the kid had been given all the lesson he could reasonably take. He was bleeding from his nose and was frozen with fear. I yelled at him to run, and it finally registered that he could escape while I was keeping his attacker busy. He vanished.

Now the man was really in a rage, and I was his new target. I watched him come at me. All the noise of the crowded street disappeared, and I saw only him and his huge fists flying toward my face in slow motion. I felt his anger, but I had no desire to hurt him. I stepped back at the exact moment his punch was to connect with my chin. He lost his balance and his huge frame made impact with thin air instead of solid flesh. With a bewildered look, he glared at me. He had punched right where I was a split second before. Like a mad bull, he charged at me with all his might. Again, I stepped aside at the moment of his full impact on my body, which was no longer there, and he toppled forward onto the broken bicycle. By this time a crowd had gathered. The big man got up quickly, ready to attack once more.

"The kid was wrong," I said, "and you taught him a lesson. I'm here to help *you*. You might have killed him if I hadn't stopped you. Let go of your anger before it makes you do something you will always regret."

He glared at me, knowing he should be able to beat me, and not understanding why he couldn't. I stood in front of him, my body relaxed, my mind resolute.

I was like the teamaster, ready to react, hoping I wouldn't have to. But there was no way he was going to fall on his knees in front of me and beg for forgiveness! He was red with rage; heat appeared to be steaming out of his whole being. I thought of running, abandoning my bike, yet I had no doubt he would be right behind me, probably following me right into my class. Wouldn't an actual demonstration surprise my students? I could hear them saying, "My ethics teacher brought a guest speaker to class; instead of debating, they fought it out."

The man stepped right in front of me, and I thought he was going to yell at me. Instead he suddenly spit right into my face. Then he turned and walked away.

Nothing ever ends as well as in a story, I thought, as I wiped the hot spit off my face. But it was okay! The young guy got away; I didn't have to hit anybody; and even the man walked away with some semblance of dignity. Getting the last shot in, I believe, gave him something he needed, and I was happy for him. I could have gone after him, given him a good kick in the groin or punch in the face as retribution. But it had turned out all right; in fact, for the twenty-first century, very well indeed!

I went to the university and taught my class, but first I washed my face more thoroughly than I have ever done in my life.

Perhaps that man sometimes thinks of me, just as I occasionally think of him. I was as enraged as he was when he spit in my face. I had a right to be. Yet I controlled my emotions, turning my anger into something positive.

The Youngest Japanese Emperor

Hojo Tokimune (1251–1284) was only seventeen years old when his father died, leaving him as supreme ruler of Japan. He governed during the period of the Mongolian Invasions. The Mongolians had already conquered China, Russia, and most of Asia. They were merciless with the people they defeated, and would cut down, maim, and torture for the slightest of excuses. Many Chinese had escaped the Mongolians by fleeing across the Western Sea into Japan, bringing tales of the horror of their occupation. Tokimune vowed that he would never see Japan under such foreign occupation, and his resistance stood as a symbol for the Japanese people for the centuries to come.

The Mongolians were amused at this "child-ruler," the inexperienced leader of a small nation, puny in size and population compared to China or Russia. Japan had only sword-wielding samurai warriors and a spirit, fueled by their young leader, that they would never be defeated.

Tokimune was sheer energy. He never stopped working, thinking, planning, and training to make himself and his nation strong. People believed in him and, through his leadership, came to believe in themselves. They looked within themselves to draw out the same energy and spirit that propelled their young ruler.

THE YOUNG EMPEROR
WHO SAVED JAPAN

Tokimune once asked Bukko, his teacher and closest adviser, "The worst enemy of our life is cowardice. How can I escape it?"

"Cut off the source from which cowardice comes," answered Bukko.

"Where does it come from?"

"It comes from Tokimune himself."

"Above all things, cowardice is what I hate most. How can it come from myself?"

"See how you feel when you throw overboard your cherished self known as Tokimune. I will see you again when you have done that."

"How can this be done?"

"Learn to shut out all your thoughts."

"How can my thoughts be shut out of consciousness?"

"Train everyday and learn to lose yourself in the process of what you are doing. Practice martial arts as a meditation-in-action, learning to focus your complete attention on the technique you are executing. When you have four attackers coming at you, become indistinguishable from them. Move as they move; think as they think. Then you will become invisible. Tokimune will no longer exist for them to defeat. If you think too much of Tokimune, you will not know them, and they will have no trouble defeating you. Learn how to block out thoughts. Become totally spontaneous, but a spontaneity which comes from disciplined training."

"I have so much to look after. I control the destiny of my country. There are so many worldly matters that I must take care of. It is difficult for me to find time for such training. There is so much else that I must do."

"Whatever worldly matters you are engaged in, even the defence of the country, make time for inner reflection. And then some day you will find out who this beloved Tokimune of yours is."

Tokimune revered Bukko. He listened closely and acted on his advice. When he finally received word that hundreds of thousands of Mongolian invaders had crossed the sea and were approaching Japan, he immediately went to see Bukko, his teacher.

"The greatest event of my life is about to take place!"

"And how do you face it?"

"*Katsu!*" Tokimune yelled fiercely, as if all his enemies were standing right before him.

"Truly a lion's child roars like a lion," Bukko said happily, realizing that Japan stood a chance. Bukko was Chinese. He had lived under the Mongolians before crossing the sea and taking refuge in Japan. He above all others knew what it would take to defeat these terrifying warriors.

This was the courage with which Tokimune faced the overwhelming force of the invaders and drove them back, and this was how a child ruler defeated an empire.

Sometimes when I am training
I become no longer me.
A thing is brought forth
I didn't know I had.
The mild man becomes the thundering lion.
And then all is quiet.

To the samurai, martial arts are the poetry of action. Tokimune discovered the lion within his being. He then went out and defeated the Mongolians: the most powerful nation on the earth – conqueror of Asia and Europe – defeated by a teenager.

VI

Thinking Outside the Box

HAKAMADARE THE THIEF CONTINUED: SAMURAI THINKING

Courage consists not in blindly overlooking danger,
but in seeing it and conquering it.

– Anonymous

Not long after his encounter with Governor Yasumasa, the famous thief Hakamadare was arrested and sent to prison. He did not stay long. An imperial pardon was passed, setting free prisoners throughout the country, including Hakamadare. Without money, a job, or clothes apart from those on his back, he had few prospects for a decent future. Thus, not altogether unhappily, he returned to a life of crime. Moreover, he had learned a great deal during his time in prison and was anxious to try out new means of theft.

He set out for Osaka, the second biggest city in Japan.

With no place to stay, and for lack of a better plan, he stripped himself naked at Osaka Barrier, a busy checkpoint on Mount Osaka. Completely unclothed, he lay down by the roadside and pretended to be dead.

Soon a crowd gathered around Hakamadare. "How on earth did he die? He doesn't have a wound! Why is he naked?"

A samurai approached from the direction of Kyoto, riding a beautiful horse and accompanied by many armed men and servants. The narrow pass was clogged with people. He stopped his horse and sent an attendant to find out what they were all looking at. The attendant returned quickly. "There is a dead man lying in the middle of the pass, sir. He has no wounds. Everyone is wondering how he died and how he got there."

The warrior ordered his men into a single file behind him and adjusted his bow and arrow. He kicked his horse and passed by, warily looking at the dead man.

The people who had gathered turned from the "dead" man to the samurai. They laughed and clapped their hands. "There goes a fierce and famous warrior and all his soldiers. He runs into a dead man and cocks his bow for protection. What a great warrior he must be!" They mocked him until he was gone from sight.

The crowd finally dispersed, leaving Hakamadare where he lay. It was late when another warrior on horseback came by. He was alone, without any servants or soldiers. He was armed with his bow and arrow. He rode up to the dead man.

"What a strange fellow. How on earth did he die? He has no wounds or signs of illness," said the samurai, as he poked at Hakamadare with the tip of his bow.

Suddenly the "dead man" grabbed the bow, jumped up, and pulled the man off his horse, knocking him out. He stripped the unconscious samurai of his clothes, donned them himself, mounted the horse, and rode away.

When Hakamadare was far enough from Osaka Barrier, he stopped to examine the beautiful swords that he had taken from the samurai. They were very old and, Hakamadare thought, must have been in the samurai's family for generations. "Now they'll remain in my family for generations to come," he said to himself realizing that now, for the first time in his life, he could imagine having a wife and children. "Dressed as I am and possessing such beautiful family swords, I will have no trouble attracting a woman who will want to have dozens of little samurai with me. But I will teach them myself how to be good samurai, not like the owner of these swords was. First though, I want retainers like that first proud samurai who passed me so cautiously on the road. That one was no fool."

His ploy had been so successful that he repeated it – thirty times. He never failed to find some fish that would fall into his net. Thus he armed and dressed thirty of his friends from prison who became his retainers. Wherever Hakamadare went, people admired the proud samurai who rode at the head of a long line of thirty loyal retainers, attentive to his every word, looking as if they owed him their very lives.

A man like Hakamadare got the better of anyone who was off his guard even slightly. A person who went near enough for him to touch was finished. Hakamadare often thought of that first samurai who so carefully rode past him, unconcerned about people laughing at him because of his prudence.

That first samurai to pass Hakamadare at Osaka Barrier was none other than the famous Taira no Sadamichi. Although he had been supported by many armed men, he knew what he knew and, as Hakamadare would joke, "could smell a rotten fish when he saw one." This warrior never allowed himself to be off guard. That was what made him such an exceptional samurai. He did not care that others called him a coward. He trusted his own instincts, and prevailed.

Musashi often used the ploy of coming late to destroy the composure of his opponents, just as he successfully did with Gan-ryu. In one situation, however, Musashi had the intuition that the ploy would not work. Therefore, he literally turned the situation on its head. Musashi always said, "Never be predictable!"

Japanese Weapons

Samurai training included skills in many weapons, such as spears and arrows, and also unarmed combat. The most prominent forms were *kendo* (the way of the sword), *kyudo* (the way of archery), *iaido* (the art of drawing the sword), and the techniques of unarmed combat that became known as *judo* (the way of gentleness) and *karate-do* (the way of the empty hand).

THE TRAP

Musashi Miyamoto was often challenged by ambitious swordsmen who were younger and stronger than he was and convinced that their youth and strength would prevail over Musashi's experience and wisdom. Unable to avoid one such match, Musashi set the time at dawn and the place beside an old Buddhist temple.

Knowing Musashi's trickery and his habit of coming late, his challenger decided to come late himself. "Let Musashi wait this time!" he said to his family and students.

"No, I have a better idea," said the man's brother. "Let's not come late. Let's arrive early. We'll hide your students in the bushes around the temple. If you're doing well, they'll just stay put and watch. If things go badly in the fight, they'll jump out and attack Musashi from behind."

"Brilliant," the samurai said. "Let's hope I won't need any help, but if I do, we'll teach Musashi a lesson in the merits of coming early and being prepared."

"The later he comes, the better," said the brother.

And so they arrived in the dark before dawn and proceeded to set themselves up according to plan. In each of the bushes beside the temple and scattered across the field they placed students armed with swords, spears, and bows. Then they all sat down to wait, the challenger and his brother alone in the middle of the large field.

A friend of Musashi had come early to watch the match and had seen the trap his challenger had prepared. No matter how many samurai were to attack him with swords and spears, Musashi's friend knew the great warrior could take them. It was the archers who worried him. They would be able to attack from a distance, free from danger, and kill Musashi before he even knew where they were hidden. He ran back down the only road to the temple and waited there to warn Musashi.

Unbeknownst to anyone, there was someone else who had arrived early. And he also was aware of all the goings-on. He was still there, in fact, hidden in one of the bushes a little farther afield, while the challenger and his brother confidently waited on the grass. That someone was Musashi Miyamoto, who had been the first to arrive – in full darkness – to watch the others, by the dim light of the pre-dawn morning sky, put their secret plan into play.

Musashi well understood that a wise strategist knows to change his plan when it gets too well-known. One must always keep one's opponents off balance and never let them know what to expect. The dawn came and went. Musashi decided to wait a little longer and let them get tired as they anxiously watched and waited. In the meantime he rested, knowing that he would have a longer fight than usual.

When Musashi judged the time to be right, when he knew that his opponents were hungry and tired from constantly watching and trying to remain composed, he ran to the nearest bush and noiselessly cut down the archer hiding there. He ran from bush to bush, taking out first the archers, then the spearmen, and finally the remaining swordsmen.

The challenger and his brother sat chatting in the field, biding their time, relaxing as they awaited the famous samurai they thought they had just outfoxed.

It's funny, Musashi thought to himself as he watched them from behind the bush where he had killed the last plotter, *how complacency destroys men. I was never complacent about Gan-ryu or anyone. I know that even my seemingly weakest opponent may have some hidden strength that I am unaware of. I am always prepared for the unexpected. Not like these two men, believing they are surrounded by their warrior companions, when in fact it is a circle of corpses that surrounds them. Except for me, of course! And now it is time to meet my appointment. I believe they are expecting me.*

Musashi jumped out from the bush, and it was as if he had fallen from the sky. His opponents could not understand how they had not even heard him walking on the noisy gravel road.

They took up fighting positions. Musashi let out his distinctive *kiai* to alert his unsuspecting friend on the road to come and watch. The man ran toward the field, fearing that Musashi was about to be skewered by spears, swords, and arrows.

Musashi took his time with his opponent, waiting for his friend to arrive. After all, the man had waited patiently alone on the road, good friend that he was. Musashi would never forget this loyalty.

Finally, the fight began. Several times Musashi drove his opponent up against the temple wall and then backed away, letting the worried man free himself. *Where are my students?* the challenger wondered. *They should have devoured Musashi by now! Isn't it evident that I won't be able to defeat Musashi on my own? What are they waiting for?*

The man charged forward with all his might, yelling out the names of his students, hoping to wake them from their slumber. Musashi smiled at the desperation on his opponent's face. He was curious to see what the expression would be when his opponent finally realized that he was all alone, that no one would come to his aid, that somehow, some way, Musashi had outfoxed him after all.

Musashi was holding back on his final thrust until the moment of supreme enlightenment would strike his opponent, like lightning from the heavens. A few seconds later, it happened, and all color drained from the man's face.

Musashi lowered his sword. "When a person confronts his own death, each moment is lived to the utmost. I dreamed of a luscious strawberry before my duel with Gan-ryu, and on the way home, in the same boat, somehow still alive, I promised myself that no strawberry would ever again be the same as before. I would savor each one, just like every experience of my life, as if it were my last. This attitude has greatly enriched my life. What do you think about that?"

The man dropped his sword and ran as fast as he could into the woods. Musashi quickly turned toward the brother, who immediately threw down his sword and followed. Musashi let them go. He had never wanted to fight this day in the first place, nor any day for that matter.

Musashi was able to get out of a trap. But it's far better to avoid a trap in the first place.

SAMURAI THINKING ON AN ELEVATOR

My daughter was coming to meet me at a friend's office in a downtown highrise. She entered the lobby of the building, and pushed the button for the elevator. When it arrived, there was a man waiting in it. My daughter thought twice about going in, and decided to wait for the next elevator, even though she was in a hurry.

She had to wait for a long time and, by the time the elevator was finally working again, it was past the hour we had arranged to meet. Always punctual, my daughter was apologetic for her lateness. But I was pleased with the choice she had made.

When should you be alert? Always – just as a samurai is always on guard. Was the man an attacker? I don't know, but I trust my daughter's intuition and am glad she had the courage to trust it too. Being late is better than putting yourself in danger.

THE SAMURAI WHO RAN AWAY

The samurai Taira no Sadatsuna and his wife were asleep when robbers broke into their house. Sadatsuna awoke as they stormed into the room. Leaping up, he reached for his sword and forced them back. Then, pushing his frightened wife ahead of him, he escaped into the courtyard. They both jumped over the cypress fence into his neighbor's yard and got away.

When people heard about this, they were shocked. "Robbers violated his house and, instead of fighting and defending his wife, he pushed her over the fence and ran away with her. Some samurai!"

Sadatsuna explained, "If the same thing were to happen again, I would act no differently. It is no heroism to risk one's life with thieves. They are desperate and will often fight to the very death. I am a samurai. It is my position to defend my country in time of crisis. That is where I will risk my life. And what if I had fought and been killed? What would have happened to my wife then? I saved us both by running. I pushed her ahead of me, protecting her as we ran."

Sadatsuna was not a coward. When war broke out, he was a brave and cunning fighter who never gave up no matter how dire the situation. He risked his life on many occasions to save others. He died in battle defending his country.

A samurai is supposed to be brave. He must be prepared to risk his life at any time. Yet he must do so only in the right circumstances. He must also know when not to risk his life. And when to run away.

The samurai, known for their courage, liked this story because it valued wisdom over bravery, as well as another samurai virtue – avoiding violence. Fight only when you have to.

OUTTHINKING THE BARRACUDA

While scuba diving in the Caribbean one early morning, I became tired from battling the rough surf.

As I turned to swim back to shore, I found myself nose-to-nose with an enormous barracuda the locals called Boris. If ever anything in my life took my breath away, it was this moment of suddenly, and completely unexpectedly, facing off with a fish that reminded me of my nightmare sharks. I wanted to go past the huge fish. How do you say excuse me to a fish? Especially a giant barracuda named Boris! He was in a playful mood and kept circling me as I tried to swim back. He was magnificent . . . but too much, too close!

I couldn't seem to lose him. He was always in front of me, or below me, or to my side – always with teeth visible. The surf was rougher than before, and I was exhausted.

I couldn't swim around Boris. So I just headed for the shore. I swam with everything I had in me and made it back, I thought, in relatively good time. I felt Boris staring at me as I climbed out of the water. I was elated and overwhelmed.

I was relieved to get back to my hotel and eat lunch with my family and friends. I was also relieved that I had not been Boris's lunch. They asked me how my morning diving had gone and I told the story.

One of my friends noted that it was a lucky thing that I was a martial artist and hence felt no fear. "No fear?" I said. "I was never so scared in my life!"

"What a disappointment!" he said. I could see that I had just dropped in everyone's opinion. "Next time you tell the story, leave out the part about being afraid, okay? It makes a much better tale."

"But I *was* afraid." I answered. "To pretend I wasn't makes it a tall tale. I didn't panic. I didn't pull out my diver's knife and confront Boris. I just swam back without making him mad."

♓

Martial arts haven't made me any less human. I think that's one of the best aspects of the samurai spirit. We will still be human even if we train to be modern-day samurai. And as humans, we will sometimes be afraid. But we can act brave. And that's a lot!

THE KING OF DEATH

It is not what happens to you
but what happens within you
that determines if you are really defeated.

– Anonymous

Two samurai were among thousands of warriors engaged in a battle that swept across a vast plain. On the overlooking hills stood hundreds of archers who rained down their arrows on the enemy soldiers.

One arrow penetrated the chest of a ferocious samurai, just above the heart. The enemy around him watched anxiously, waiting to see if anything could really halt the warrior who killed so many of their bravest men. The wounded man saw the arrow piercing his body and dropped his sword as he staggered, trying to pull the arrow out. The men around him fell on him from all sides, and in seconds he was dead.

Across the same plain, a second powerful samurai was also struck by a falling arrow, which hit him in the exact same place as the first arrow hit the ferocious samurai. This warrior's opponents could not believe their luck. They closed in for the kill, being careful to wait to see if he was truly felled. The warrior looked at the arrow sticking out of his body, grabbed his sword with two hands over his head, let out a tremendous, ear-shattering *kiai*, and continued his relentless advance on the enemy.

Seeing the ashen warrior advancing toward them with the arrow sticking out of his chest, and hearing his voice that seemed to come from the underworld, they scattered, as if being chased by the King of Death.

In a few moments, with no one left around him to fight, the wounded samurai sat down to rest. A comrade removed the arrow and dressed the wound. This samurai lived to fight many more battles, with a ferocious scar on his chest just above the heart and an awe-inspiring nickname: the King of Death.

What killed the first warrior? Was it the first arrow? Or was it really the second arrow – the one he inflicted upon himself – the arrow of despair?

Perhaps the greatest lesson of the samurai is not that we should never feel fear, but that we should never give in to it.

When others may quit and despair, those with the samurai spirit maintain the energy, the spirit, and the focus to find the way around every obstacle. Life isn't just what happens to us but, more importantly, how we react to it.

VII
Making a Difference in the World

*If it looks like wisdom,
but is unkind rather than loving,
it is not wisdom.*

– Lama Surya Das

The samurai tradition provides a foundation for justice by empowering each of us to contribute, by our actions, born of our own personal development, to creating a better world.

THE EIGHTY-YEAR-OLD SAMURAI

Masanari had lived a long and glorious life as a respected samurai. Even in old age, he was kept in the employ of his lord. However, Masanari lived far longer than most people at that time were accustomed to, and he decided to find a place where he could still be of use.

He was hired as a guard at a Buddhist monastery near a quiet lake. He was happy living among the monks, who kept him company in his old age while he protected them.

One day, a rowdy drunk appeared outside the gates of the monastery, brandishing his sword and chasing visitors away. He kicked at the gates, he slashed trees with his sword, and he threatened to burn down the monastery if the monks didn't come out. The monks were terrified.

Suddenly the temple gate flew open and out hobbled Masanari, supporting himself with a cane.

"You're dressed as a samurai," the drunken man said. "But where are your swords, old man?"

"I'm too old to carry them. They're too heavy for me," he smiled. Was he mocking the younger man or was he serious?

The drunk, obviously a former samurai himself, could not stop laughing. "This is the best that the monks can do – hire an old man who can no longer hold a sword to guard their monastery? This place deserves to be burned down!"

He lifted his sword to cut down the old man, but as the sword swept down, the old man dodged and grabbed the drunk's arm. The old samurai twisted so hard that the attacker dropped his sword, just as the old man swept his feet out from under him. The old samurai threw the sword in the lake and slowly hobbled back inside. The monks watched in awe as the old warrior returned to his room to rest.

At eighty years old, he had just defeated, without weapons, an attacker with a sword. Only then did the monks muster their courage and come out and carry the unconscious man away.

A man of few words, Masanari never told his son this story. Yet nothing in his life was more astonishing than this incident from his old age.

> ### *Passing on the Samurai Spirit*
> The samurai Arai Hakuseki (1657–1725) attained the position of chief counselor to the shogun. He was a very learned man who wrote a well-known book, a lively portrait of his samurai father, Masanari.
>
> It is interesting that often we know little about the lives of our fathers or mothers until they are dead and others tell us about them. Hakuseki writes beautifully about how he regretted not knowing his father better before he succumbed to illness and death. He writes that, many years after his father's death, a Buddhist monk told him this story about his father.
>
> "I didn't have a chance to see your father when he was young," said the monk. "When he was past eighty, however, I had occasion to see him in action right in front of my eyes." Hakuseki's father was a warrior who lost neither his strength nor his ideals. Even at eighty, even after his death, he still had a lesson or two to pass on to his learned son.

THE GIFT THAT COULD
NOT BE STOLEN

Shichiri Kojun was seated in evening meditation at his small house on the outskirts of town. The house was dark, for Shichiri had no need of light during meditation, or for the martial arts practice he had just finished. For over fifty years, he had practiced the martial arts diligently. Even now, no longer in the prime of his life, he never missed a day of training.

Seeing no light and hearing no noise from within, a passing robber thought that the house was an ideal place to finish his lucrative evening's work. He unsheathed his long sword and crept into the house.

"You are making too much noise," a voice called out. "My money is in a silk purse uder the tatami mat."

Through the darkness, the thief saw a man seated motionless on a cushion in the adjacent room. He found the purse, and in it was a small pile of money. "Don't take it all. I have to pay my bills tomorrow," the seated man called out. "And ask politely when you want something."

"May I have some money?" the thief asked, surprising himself.

"Yes," Shichiri replied.

The thief took half the coins and put the rest back. "Thank

a person when he gives you a gift," the voice called out again. Without understanding why he was doing so, the thief obeyed the man and thanked him, then bowed, and quickly ran out of the house and down the street leading to the woods outside of town.

Later that night, the thief was caught. The authorities made every attempt to return the stolen items to their owners and to collect statements concerning the guilt of their prisoner. Shichiri was the last to be consulted, since all that was stolen from him was money, and it was difficult to tell from whom it had been taken. A neighbor said he had seen a man running from Shichiri's house that evening. The authorities knocked at the samurai's door, explaining that they had his stolen money.

Shichiri responded. "As far as I am concerned, this man is no thief. He came into my house and politely asked for money. I gave it to him. He thanked me for it. If he were indeed a thief, he would have taken the rest of my money." Shichiri drew the string on the silk purse and showed the coins still in it. "He is an unfortunate man, poorer than I. I wish I could have given him something more. I wish I could have taught him how to appreciate the beauty of the moon." Shichiri motioned toward the sky where the full moon was glowing.

Several years later, when the thief had finished his prison term, he sought out Shichiri. "I see you want to learn how to appreciate the beauty of the moon," the old man said when he saw the former thief. He looked not the least bit surprised or disturbed – no more than he had that first night when the man broke into his house.

The man who had been a burglar studied devotedly with Shichiri until the day that the master died.

The money Shichiri gave the burglar could not be stolen, because it was a gift. The samurai was so generous that he wanted to give the thief an even greater gift, the ability to appreciate the beauty of the moon, the wonder of the things we see around us everyday that have a value beyond money.

Ideals in an Imperfect World

Musashi Miyamoto became wise, turning his back on the shallow ambition of defeating others and concentrating on improving himself. But he knew that the world was a dangerous place, full of wars and famine, and that even in peacetime rogues exist. Peace and relative prosperity had arrived in Japan many years before, but it was still necessary to train just as hard as in war, in order to live in peace.

Musashi hoped that his own life would inspire others to train hard and pursue the arts in order to develop themselves and create a better world. He knew a better world comes not just from high ideals, but also the personal power to pursue these ideals.

THE IMPATIENT STUDENT

Maturity is the ability to make a decision and stand by it.
The immature spend their lives exploring endless possibilities;
then they do nothing.

– Anonymous

A samurai felt he could do nothing more with his son, who showed neither interest nor aptitude for learning swordsmanship. He sent the young man to be an apprentice to a well-known samurai who lived alone on a remote mountain.

"How long do I have to stay here?" the young man asked as soon as he arrived.

"Let me ask you a question," the samurai replied. "How long do you think you need to learn how to grasp the art of the sword?"

"I don't know, maybe two to three years? What do you think?"

"I would say ten to twenty years."

"That's too long." The young man was shocked. "I am anxious to return to my father to show him how great a samurai I can be. What if I study really hard?"

"Thirty years!"

"What? What if I study night and day without ever leaving, even for vacations?"

"Forty years!"

"That doesn't make sense. The harder I study, the more time it takes?"

"The more impatient you are, the harder it is to learn anything quickly. Now let's forget about this. Get unpacked and we will start. I promised your father that I would try to teach you something. No more talk about swordsmanship or martial arts. Let's get to work."

The young man unpacked and prepared himself for his first fencing lesson, laying out his training outfit and all his equipment.

"Come down for supper," the master called out.

The master was getting the pot and the utensils ready. "Wash the rice in the stream," he said. After the rice was washed, the master told his student to go to the well to get some fresh water to cook the rice in. "Now set the table." After supper, the master quickly started clearing the table. "Wash the dishes," he said. After the dishes were all washed and the room cleaned, the master gave his student a futon. "Make your bed and go to sleep."

Early the next morning, the master woke the young man and told him to prepare quickly for breakfast. "Wash the rice," he instructed. "Now draw fresh water from the well, then set the table." After breakfast, the master told him to wash the dishes. When the young man finished that, he was given a broom and told to sweep up the house and the outside courtyard. Then the master told him it was time for lunch. "Wash the rice," he said. After cleanup, the student was given a hoe and told to work in the garden. A few hours later, he was again told to wash the rice for supper. After that, it was cleanup and time for bed.

The next morning, the young man was once again awakened at an early hour and told to wash the rice . . . and the day went exactly as the day before. After breakfast he was given the broom, and then a few hours later told to wash the rice for lunch. After cleanup, he was given the hoe for the vegetable garden, until he was told to wash the rice for supper. After cleanup, he did not need to be told to go to bed. He fell into bed himself and into an immediate deep sleep.

This routine continued for several weeks. Finally the young man could contain himself no longer and spoke up to the master: "What about the fencing lessons that I was sent here to receive?"

"I never saw any real interest or enthusiasm in you to learn martial arts."

"Anything beats this," the young man answered.

"Is that so?" responded the master, throwing him the broom.

As the young student was sweeping up, annoyed at having his wishes and questions ignored, out of nowhere the master swept his feet right out from under him, sending him sprawling to the ground. By the time he got up, the master was gone. He wasn't sure that he had seen the master at all, but somebody obviously had swept his legs out from under him. Who else could it have been? They were miles from anywhere.

Later, while he was washing the rice, he felt a strong blow to his upper back. It sent him flying. The rice spilled on the ground. When he turned around, no one was there. While he was washing the dishes, someone slapped him with a bamboo stick in between his shoulder blades. He turned to see the master quietly putting the clean dishes away.

The next day, the sweep, the blow, the stick – it all happened again. The student had no doubt it was his master, but he never actually saw the samurai do anything. By the time he turned around, he was alone, or the master was there busily doing something else. This continued for weeks. He regretted that he had ever come to talk to the master about learning martial arts. The only thing that resulted from that conversation was that he was continually getting beaten up. Some martial arts training that was! He spoke once again to the master, but the attacks only got worse. He was constantly struck, knocked off his feet, or sent sprawling to the ground.

One day, the student came into the house unexpectedly to get a garden tool. He saw the master, with his back turned, stirring something in the big dinner pot. His heart soared. He grabbed the bamboo training sword leaning against the wall and silently crept up behind the master. Ah, it was so pleasant to turn the tables!

He lifted the sword and brought it down as hard and fast as he could on the master's left shoulder. Quick as lightning, the master lifted a pot cover over his shoulder, effectively blocking the blow. Then, without even turning around, he gently placed the cover back on the big pot.

The young man crept from the room astounded at what had just happened. Did the master consciously block the blow? Was it humanly possible for anyone to move so fast? The master did not say anything or even turn around. He showed no anger, as if to say, "Why would I be the least bit upset about that young man trying to smash me from behind with a bamboo sword? That's no threat for me!"

The apprentice decided to learn to emulate the master. He would try to be aware at every moment of what was happening around him, so that he would be prepared to block a blow, right out of the blue.

At first, nothing much changed. Yet with time he found himself imitating the master's constant mindfulness. Sometimes he succeeded in moving aside at the moment of the sweep or in dodging the blows at his back. After several months, he was successful almost half the time. He tried harder. He observed the master, relentlessly trying to imitate every detail of each of his actions, of his very being. He would get up early and watch the master practicing his martial arts, and then quietly slip off into the woods and imitate the master's movements.

The years passed, and the apprentice improved. His heightened awareness made him focus on each moment. He began to enjoy his gardening, his cooking, and even his sweeping and rice washing. Every moment counted to him as his awareness of the world around him deepened.

He also became more effective in his blocks and dodges, so effective that the master began to teach him how to improve. The apprentice grew to appreciate the master's words and attention, and soon began to show it, saying "Thank you, sir," after being taught something. The master in turn complimented his apprentice on his growing abilities and his heightened consciousness.

One day the master came into his student's room and told him that it was time for him to leave. His father was ill and needed him at home. The apprentice was now a true samurai and, with pride, could take over his father's activities. Reluctantly he prepared to leave and said his heartfelt farewells to his master.

Where at first he hadn't wanted to come, now he didn't want to go.

Confronting the constant attacks from his master, the young man came to realize that his master's ability to so effectively block even surprise attacks was based upon his serenity, his mindfulness, and his lack of fear. The master's attitude seemed to say, "Whatever happens to me in life, I am ready, and I am strong enough to face it." The samurai was not simply a master of the martial arts. Being that made him truly a master of life.

There is something to be learned from a rainstorm.
When meeting with a sudden shower, you try not to get wet
and run quickly along the road.
By doing such things as passing under the eaves of houses,
you still get wet.
When you are resolved from the beginning,
you will not be perplexed, though you will
still get the same soaking.
This understanding extends to all things.

– from the *Hagakure*

A Samurai Is One Who Serves

The samurai class of Japan saw in the ancient teaching of Buddha a powerful means of training their minds in order to perfect their physical technique and focus their concentration. They could thus increase the chances of their survival in battle and of finding happiness in their personal lives.

There was a further element of Buddha's teaching that appealed to the samurai. It was a sense of responsibility – that each person had an important role in enhancing his or her own life, but also an obligation to use this personal strength to relieve the suffering of others. This gave great meaning to the life of a samurai, whose entire existence was based upon developing his strength and skill, as well as his readiness to die, in order to protect the community around him.

For Daruma, the Buddhist monk who was instrumental in the development of the martial arts, strength was the foundation of helping others. Daruma believed that it took more than high ideals to create a better world and alleviate suffering. Of course, they were necessary, but so was physical strength and spirit. A motto of this type of training developed in Japan several hundred years after Daruma: *bunbu-ryodo*, the combination of intellectual and martial training.

THE TEST

It is the battle within ourselves
that brings out our true worth.

– Samurai proverb

I had proudly volunteered to be in a martial arts demonstration with my *sensei*. I was going to have a school examination later that day, but it was going to be an easy one and I knew that my help was needed at the demonstration.

However, the night before the demonstration, I was feeling ill. I had eaten one slice of pizza too many, and was sick to my stomach. I called the *dojo* early the next morning, hoping that another student could take my place.

"You don't have to speak," said Sensei. "All I need is someone to assist me. I'm not asking you to do too much. I'm counting on you."

Sensei had taught us the importance of always keeping our word. He had certainly chosen the right words to motivate me. No matter how I was feeling, I didn't want to let him down.

I got changed and went to the *dojo* to meet Sensei. It was a big demonstration before an audience of about 500. Several junior students were there, but I was the only one at an advanced level. It was true; Sensei needed me. I said I would introduce my teacher and say a few words about martial arts. There was a microphone, so I didn't have to speak too loudly. It wouldn't be too hard. It might be all I could do, but it would be enough.

The audience was unexpectedly enthusiastic. As I briefly

explained the history and philosophy of the martial arts, they listened attentively. The beginners did a very good job of demonstrating their skills. Sensei was, as usual, superb. Things were really cooking! We were all excited, catching the enthusiasm of the spectators.

Sensei set up some boards and bricks to demonstrate the power of karate kicks and punches. Then, instead of breaking them himself, he introduced me as one of his advanced and promising students who, even though not feeling well, would illustrate the spirit of a martial artist by breaking the board and bricks. I came forward and broke the boards, first with a kick and then with an elbow strike.

Then it was time to break the brick with a punch. I had never tried before and, my body still aching from last night's pizza binge, I wasn't prepared. I stood in front of the brick. I paused to concentrate, trying to focus my energy, but couldn't. I looked at the audience, quiet in anticipation. My head throbbed, and my legs felt weak underneath me. I was unable to block out the 500 people watching me, the pounding in my head, the shaking of my legs.

I turned into the punch and thrust forward with my fist. The audience gasped. My knuckles smashed into the brick at tremendous velocity, and I felt a burning pain spread through my hand. The brick was still there, mocking me, victorious over my swollen hand and shattered spirit.

My friends tried to reassure me before Sensei came over. "It wasn't fair," they kept repeating. "He shouldn't have made you do it. Why didn't he just break them himself?" I was too exhausted to respond. Besides, I didn't know the answer.

"What happened there?" asked Sensei firmly, looking straight into my eyes. "You can do it. You know you can. You are my student, and I taught you how to be a true samurai. Now get out there and break that brick!"

My friends glared at Sensei as I returned to the stage. Sensei held the brick. I took my stance, focused my energy, blocked out my throbbing head, breathed deeply from my lower abdomen, drew on the force of my legs, and thrust my fist right through the brick, turning it into powder. The audience cheered, but I didn't hear them. I was still deep in concentration.

Slowly, my awareness of everything returned, and I saw Sensei smiling at me. He was right – he had taught me to be a true samurai, and I had not let him down.

"It wasn't for me that you did this," he explained. "I could have done it myself. You did this for you! Now, for the rest of your life, you will know what you are made of.

Ħ

Sensei saw used this opportunity to help me see an important truth. He shared with me the demonstration that mattered – a demonstration of the nature of the samurai spirit.

THE MONK WITH A PUNCH

I believe in mountains;
They are a practical reminder of how high I must reach.

– Anonymous

In the mountains outside of Kyoto lived Butsugai, a monk in a Zen Buddhist temple. Like the others in the monastery, Butsugai wore robes and had a shaved head. He was also good natured, like most monks. They all worked hard to live up to the traditions of Daruma. They gave up marriage and worldly possessions to live simple lives in the monastery. Their days were spent in study and labor in their vegetable gardens. Vegetarians, they ate simple but ample meals and always shared their food with those in need.

Butsugai was a true warrior. The son of a samurai, he practiced martial arts rigorously every day. He was lean and muscular, although this was well hidden under the loose robes and ready smile of the monk. Immensely strong, he could punch a hole in just about anything. That is how he earned his nickname, the Monk with a Punch.

In Butsugai's time Japan suffered from civil strife and the rise of roving gangs who took power in certain districts. Kyoto was taken over by one such warrior gang of rowdy and violent swordsmen who terrorized the people.

Butsugai set out for Kyoto. The *sensei* at the monastery had warned him to learn what he could about the warriors, but to avoid confrontations with them. If any trouble developed, he should return to the monastery to seek help. With this advice clearly in mind, Butsugai entered the city and, by chance, passed directly in front of the gang's headquarters. Attracted by the sounds of martial arts *kiai* and of bamboo swords clashing, Butsugai found a window and looked in.

The men saw that Butsugai was watching them. They demanded to know why he was spying. Butsugai apologized, explaining that he was only a Buddhist monk who had come out of the mountains. The men decided to have some fun with a hapless country monk.

"You must know something about the martial arts to be watching us like that. Come inside and duel with us."

Butsugai tried to refuse, but they would not let go of the fun they were about to have with him. The men took up bamboo swords, ready to attack the ragged monk one after another. Without showing the slightest fear, Butsugai took his simple walking stick and effortlessly smashed down the sword of each attacker. All the gang members joined in and, in a matter of minutes, Butsugai had disposed of several dozen attackers.

Furious, the leader of the gang stepped up, carrying a long spear. "Your skills are too great for these youngsters," he said, "but I, Kondo Isamu, challenge you to a fight."

Butsugai fell to the ground in a position of utmost humility. He begged pardon for having to act in self-defence. "I have heard of you, Kondo Isamu. They call you the genius of the martial arts. How could a wandering monk like me be any match for someone like you? Please let me go. I am hardly worthy to be your opponent."

Emboldened by the monk's words, Kondo demanded that Butsugai choose a weapon. "I am a Buddhist monk," Butsugai replied, "I will not pick up weapons. My walking stick will do to support me." But still Kondo insisted that the monk choose a weapon.

Butsugai reached into the pockets of his robe and pulled out a pair of wooden rice bowls. Gripping one in each hand, he smiled. "I am ready."

Infuriated, the fighter was determined to wipe out his opponent with a single thrust. Gripping his spear, he readied himself for the attack.

But Kondo could find no opening in Butsugai's unusual defence. The minutes passed, without Kondo moving even an eyelid, as Butsugai slowly and deliberately waved his rice bowls in front of him. Butsugai's movements were hypnotic, his smile unwavering, his stances graceful and controlled. Finally Kondo saw an opening. He thrust his spear at Butsugai with enough power to skewer the monk to the far wall.

Butsugai dodged the attack and trapped the spear between the two rice bowls. There it remained, held solidly in a vise-like grip. Pulling and pushing with everything he had, Kondo could not wrest his spear free from the powerful grip of the monk's bowls. Soon he was completely soaked in sweat. Butsugai, smiling broadly, effortlessly held fast to the spear.

Finally Butsugai released the spear – at the precise moment that Kondo pulled back with all his might. Kondo fell back, his spear flying behind him. Kondo picked himself up from the floor and looked Butsugai in the eyes. "Who are you?" he asked, "to be able to do such things as I have never before seen?"

"I am the wandering monk called Butsugai," the Zen man replied.

"Ah, so you are the famous Monk with a Punch!" exclaimed Kondo. "You should wear a sign, you know."

"Wait until you see my students, who will be with me when I return tomorrow."

Kondo and his gang of warriors quickly and quietly left Kyoto the next morning, allowing the people to live in peace.

When Butsugai finished his Zen studies at the monastery, he went to live in seclusion to meditate, practice, and study. Soon people sought him out for instruction in Zen or the martial arts. One day a renowned swordsman came to study with him.

"Why have you come here?" Butsugai asked.

"I have come to die at the teacher's fists."

Butsugai was so impressed with this answer that he allowed the young samurai to stay and study with him. Later Butsugai presented him with a verse:

Even the power of the Howling Spirit –
A single layer of mosquito netting.

Like all Japanese poems, this one has many possible meanings. One thing it reveals is the essence of the martial arts – its intrinsic gentleness. The Monk with a Punch taught the younger samurai that, if you have true samurai spirit, even the most ferocious of challenges can be as deftly handled as if it was simply a layer of mosquito netting.

At the heart of the samurai spirit is the ability to be flexible, not hard. In a windstorm, maple and oak trees will stand stiff and immovable, resisting the force of the wind – until they break. After the storm, the forest floor will be littered with their broken branches. A pine tree seems to be weaker than these hardwood trees, but its branches are flexible. They bend in the wind and do not break. The pine tree is an enduring symbol of the true samurai spirit, that of Butsugai and the many other wise warriors in the samurai tradition.

THE DILEMMA

Zenkai, born of a samurai family, received his first position as a retainer to a high official in Tokyo. He was excited, not only about his position, but also to be in the big city, where he was sure great adventure awaited him.

Much to his disappointment, he found his duties to be mostly administrative and boring. They left him with little free time to get out into the city and make friends. Where was the exciting life he had dreamed of?

Being a high official, Zenkai's employer had to travel, and Zenkai often found himself alone with the older samurai's wife and baby. The woman was far younger than her husband, and Zenkai fell in love with her. One day her husband returned home unexpectedly and found them together. He drew his sword, but the younger and stronger samurai easily killed the furious husband in self-defence. Knowing he would be put to death for his act, Zenkai ran away with the wife.

Needless to say, Zenkai couldn't get a good reference for new employment from his old employer. He became a thief and did very well at his new profession. But as his woman became increasingly greedy, Zenkai regretted taking her from her husband. Finally Zenkai left her, journeying to the far away province of Buzen.

After years of wandering and scavenging for food and shelter, he began to think about what had happened to his life. He had been born a samurai! How had he ended up like this, a common thief, living no better than an animal? Where were his high ideals in *bushido*, the code of ethics of the samurai?

The best thing, he thought, would be to kill himself – to save some other samurai the trouble of doing so, and to protect others from having to make his unfortunate acquaintance. He was worthless! He had already brought so much trouble into the world: killing one man, stealing his wife, robbing others. The sooner he could use his sword upon himself, the better off the world would be.

Just at that moment as he was walking, caught up in his thoughts, he found himself right at the edge of a high cliff. Looking down, he realized he didn't need to use his sword to end his life – he didn't deserve to die by its blade, anyway. He need only jump onto the jagged rocks far below. Looking down, he saw the remains of wagons and skeletons of horses and humans who had obviously fallen from the twisting, treacherous road he was traveling.

A young woman suddenly grabbed him in a powerful grip,

and led him away from the edge of the cliff. "You mustn't go so close," she told him, "Enough people have already lost their lives to this road."

"Isn't there another path they can take?" Zenkai asked.

"No," the woman answered. "This is the only way into or out of the village. This is our lifeline."

Astonished, Zenkai looked up to see people, some with babies or children in their arms, trying to climb up the cliff. Some led animals loaded with goods. He feared that the very people he was watching would fall to their deaths, babies and animals and children and all. He wanted to cry.

He looked at the strong young woman who was gazing respectfully at him. *Why*, he asked himself, *is she looking at me like that? Doesn't she see how horrible I am?* Then he looked down and saw that, despite the scruffy face and unkempt hair, he was still wearing the dress of a samurai and carrying his two swords.

He faced a choice. He could jump off the cliff and kill himself, saving humanity from further harm. But he would also be saving himself from the horror of having to reflect on what he had become. Or he could take a harder way out. He could do something to atone for his past. He could accomplish some good deed in his lifetime.

This cliff has cost the lives of hundreds of people, he said to himself. *If I resolve to build a new path, cutting a tunnel through the mountain, I could save thousands of people. I could cause happiness instead of death and sorrow! I could more than make up for the one man I have killed and the many others I have robbed!*

And so he did. Begging food in the daytime, Zenkai worked during the night. His swords lying by his side, he took up shovel and pick with the same enthusiasm with which he had performed the martial arts exercises of his youth. By the time thirty years had passed, his tunnel was almost a mile long, high and wide enough for several people to walk through it side-by-side. In another two years, Zenkai was certain, it would be finished.

✄

One day, a man sat down near Zenkai and watched him dig away at the tunnel. Day after day, the man came to sit and watch patiently.

Finally one morning Zenkai approached the man and asked what he wanted, why he was there every day, watching silently. As soon as he got close to the man, however, Zenkai knew the answer. He saw anger in the man's eyes, the same anger, the same eyes he had seen in the official's bedroom that morning he was discovered with the man's wife. This was the son of the samurai he had killed so many years ago.

"And I know who you are," the man said when he saw that Zenkai had recognized him. He had his hands on his swords as he spoke.

"You must be a very good samurai to have tracked me so far from Tokyo. It is a miracle that you ever found me."

"I was a babe in arms when you killed my father and ran away with my mother. My grandparents raised me as a good samurai. I was taught that when I grew up, I must search for my father's killer and mete out justice according to samurai tradition. The elders of this province have assured me that I have both the legal and moral right, as well as responsibility, to kill you as punishment for what you did to my father and

128

to our family. I am thirty-two years old, and I have trained my whole life for this day."

The younger samurai slowly removed his sword from the scabbard. Zenkai instinctively reached for his own, but realized he had left it at the mouth of the tunnel. He knew he didn't need it anyway. He was not going to fight the son of the man he had killed. He had long ago resigned himself to death. But why now, just when he was so close to finishing something so good? Why now?

Zenkai fell on his knees before the man. "I will give you my life freely, without struggle. You deserve your revenge. I deserve my punishment. Only please let me finish this work, which I have started in order to atone for what I did to your father. Let many others live because your father has died. Let that be a part of your justice. On the day the tunnel is finished, then you may kill me."

The official's son waited that day, and the next. He didn't mind. He had waited thirty years. Months passed. Zenkai kept on digging. One day, the son grew tired of watching and began to help, in order to hasten the day of justice. With the two of them working, it went much faster than Zenkai had imagined and, after about a year, they were very close to completing the tunnel.

The official's son had come to admire Zenkai's strong will and character, his dedication to the task. "He has the same determination as I," the son thought. "How odd that we should be so similar."

Finally the tunnel was completed, and there was a great celebration. The townspeople honored Zenkai for his gift, conferred with thirty years of his life and labor.

Zenkai approached the young man. Bowing deeply, he said, "Now cut off my head. My work is done." The younger samurai drew out his sword. He looked at the man lying prostrate before him. He hesitated.

"Hurry up," Zenkai yelled. "I'm getting cold waiting for you!"

What should I do? the samurai asked himself. *I am here to deliver justice, but what is most just? Do I kill the murderer as he deserves, as he himself demands? But this is not the same man as the one who killed my father. What will my killing him accomplish? What other wonderful things is he yet capable of doing to help others? Especially if I will be there to help him!*

The samurai dropped to his knees beside Zenkai and lowered his sword. "How can I cut off my own teacher's head?" asked the samurai with tears in his eyes.

RECOMMENDED READING

Cleary, Thomas, *The Japanese Art of War*. Boston: Shambhala, 1992.

Cleary, Thomas, *Zen Antics*. Boston: Shambhala, 1993.

Das, Surya, *Awakening the Buddha Within*. New York: Broadway Books, Bantam Doubleday, 1997.

Fauliot, Pascal, *Martial Arts Teaching Tales*. Rochester, Vermont: Inner Traditions, 2000.

Hyams, Joe, *Zen in the Martial Arts*. New York: Bantam Books, 1979.

King, Winston, *Zen and the Way of the Sword*. New York: Oxford University Press, 1993.

Konzak, Burt, *Noguchi the Samurai*. Toronto: Lester Publishing, 1994.

Konzak, Burt, *Girl Power: Self-Defence for Teens*. Toronto: Sport Books Publisher, 1999.

Mishima, Yukio, *The Way of the Samurai*. New York: Basic Books, 1977.

Ross, Nancy Wilson, *The World of Zen*. New York: Vintage Books, Random House, 1960.

Sato, Hiroaki, *Legends of the Samurai*. Woodstock: Overlook Press, 1995.

Yoshikawa, Eiji, *Musashi*. New York: Kodansha, 1971.

Suzuki, D.T., *Zen and Japanese Culture*. Princeton: Princeton University Press, 1959.

In addition, the following films directed by Akira Kurosawa are available on videotape: *Judo Saga* part I (1943), *Rashomon* (1950), *Seven Samurai* (1954), *Red Beard* (1965), *Ran* (1985). Kurosawa went to great lengths to accurately portray samurai culture and spirit.